THE GURUGU PLEDGE

THE GURUGU PLEDGE

Juan Tomás Ávila Laurel

Translated by Jethro Soutar

SHEFFIELD – LONDON – NEW HAVEN

First published by And Other Stories
Sheffield – London – New Haven
www.andotherstories.org

9 8 7 6 5 4 3 2 1

ISBN: 978-1-908276-94-0
eBook ISBN: 978-1-908276-95-7

Editors: Stefan Tobler and Jethro Soutar; Proofreader: Sarah Terry; Typesetter: Tetragon, London; Typefaces: Linotype Swift Neue and Verlag; Cover Design: Edward Bettison. Cover photograph: Samuel Aranda, reproduced courtesy of Panos Pictures. Printed and bound by the CPI Group (UK) Ltd, Croydon, CR0 4YY.

A catalogue record for this book is available from the British Library.

This book has been selected to receive financial assistance from English PEN's PEN Translates! programme. English PEN exists to promote literature and our understanding of it, to uphold writers' freedoms around the world, to campaign against the persecution and imprisonment of writers for stating their views, and to promote the friendly co-operation of writers and the free exchange of ideas. www.englishpen.org

And Other Stories is also supported using public funding by Arts Council England.

Supported using public funding by
ARTS COUNCIL
ENGLAND

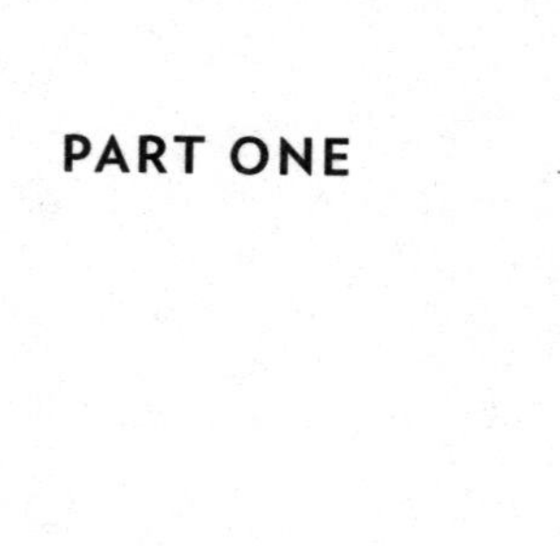

PART ONE

I

We lived in the forest and cooked enough to still be standing. We gathered firewood and went down into Farkhana to buy fish, or to pretend to buy fish in the hope that some charitable soul would give us some. Of course, if they did, it would always be the least substantial part, such as the head or the bones. But it would provide a little nourishment and warmth, and it was cold in the residence, much colder than on the banks of the River Ruo, where I was born, and saw others born, those I left behind to go in search of new rivers, different riverbanks. After eating, assuming there was anything to eat, we warmed our hands over the fire, curled up on our cardboard, or under our blankets, and settled down to listen to people's stories. I always acted as though I had no story to tell, as though I had nothing to say. The fact of the matter was that if I'd started to talk, if I'd started to tell of all the things I'd seen and the tales I'd heard, I'd never have stopped. People would have thought it was custom among my people not to allow others to talk and they'd have heard my voice tremble besides and thought me an artist trying to mislead them. So I kept my mouth shut and listened to those who were kind enough to share their stories.

There was nothing to be cheerful about in the residence, so anyone able to step outside their immediate reality and speak of something other than the day-to-day was considered a hero. Yes, a hero, because we had ample cause to complain, to curse our luck from morning till night, and yet when the time came to stick hands between thighs and try to get some sleep, a few good folk always found the strength to speak of what their lives had been before coming to the residence.

Good folk like Peter. He had a beard from never shaving and he told us that in his village he'd been known as Ngambo. He said he'd once been a porter, though he didn't say what of or who for; it was enough that he'd agreed to share his story. Ngambo told us he never intended to leave his country, he'd only done so because his father had been discriminated against. Whenever he mentioned his father he sat up, to make sure the details were understood, to make sure the man's extraordinary good character was never in doubt. He didn't want to overemphasise his father's importance, he said, but he did want to make sure the details were properly understood.

Peter's father first cropped up one night after dinner had been served and the remains cleared away. You, lad, keep an eye on the fire, and be careful because if it gets out of control, we're all doomed, but if it goes out, the wolves will come and steal our babies: the fire represents our present and future.

'What present and future?' one of the residents asked.

'The babies, of course.'

'Don't be silly,' said someone else, 'there are no wolves left on this mountain.'

'No wolves left?'

'If there were any wolves left, do you think we'd be wasting our money on frozen chicken, eh? Have you seen any sign of animal life in this forest?'

'You can't eat wolf, brother. As for chicken, I appreciate the sentiment, but in all my time here I've only ever seen a pair of chicken feet being barbecued, although I never got to taste them, so I assume you mention buying frozen chicken just to brighten up our day, for which I thank you.'

'You can eat wolf, just not in a residence like this, with no water or electricity. As for the chicken, that's in God's hands, but if I've brightened up your day, my pleasure.'

'I'm still not convinced. How do you even catch a wolf, eh?'

'If you have to ask that question, brother, you've never known true hunger.'

'Look, never mind all this. Peter was about to tell us the story of his father, the reason why he's here among us. Go on, brother Peter, thank you for your patience.'

'Yes, go on, Peter,' someone else cut in, 'tell us why you're here and not in an embassy somewhere, somewhere without a dictatorship, working as a sports attaché or whatever.'

'I want to make it clear, first and foremost, that it was not my father's fault, it was envy, the envy of everyone around him. The envy and ignorance that exists in all black people. Whenever I hear a white person talk about the ignorance of black people, my heart aches, this heart I have right here, and I close my eyes so as not to have to listen to what they are saying. But I also know that we have given them reason to say it, and until we show them any different, what is written in books will be what continues to be read out on the radio, day and night.'

That's how Peter started his story, having been prompted to do so by a fellow resident. He waited for a few seconds, to see if there was any resistance, and then, once he was confident everyone was listening, even those with their eyes closed, he began.

His father had been a pupil in a French lycée. He'd been born in a country with English-language customs, a country where they even wore grey wigs in court, the better to uphold ancient traditions, but where it was the fashion to send children to French school, and so there he'd been sent, and there he'd learned canon law, which would suggest he was being prepared for the priesthood. If he had become a priest, there would have been no story to tell, for there would have been no Peter: his father would have led a life of celibacy and avoided all women. Or maybe not all of them, but we would never have known about it, for his story would never have reached the residence. But that's to speak of what might have been and what might have been was turned on its head by a poem. Yes, a simple poem, for while attending that school, the French lycée, Peter's father found himself immersed in a culture that allowed him to declare himself a poet of the Conceptismo movement. Or maybe there was no such cultural dynamic, maybe Peter's father took it upon himself to launch and join his own cultural movement, but no matter, the important thing is he wrote a poem, and, according to what Peter remembered, it went something like this:

Charon, bring hither that boat,
we'll away to the lake's end,
reach the exact point of femininity,
door-knocker of revolution above.

You, Charon, ready that boat's reins,
we'll cross swiftly and tap
the point whence the jealous wail and cry to the heathen
eunuch, enclosed in the palace in false faithfulness.

For if you bring it, Charon, the drooling
eunuch will break his troth, a thousand
and one gilliflower virgins will succumb to his charms
and godly battle will wage on high.

That's where the poem ended, at least the version we were told. And that should have been the end of the matter, except that Peter's father had declared himself a Conceptist poet and so he'd included a gloss to unlock the poem. That should still have been that, but the poem, which he'd written in French, keen student that he was, and the gloss, which he'd written in English, fell into the hands of the prefect, as the dean in charge of discipline at that school was called. The prefect was local, a native of that country where English was the chosen language, or the imposed language, imposed by rich whites, but he knew how to be very French, very dry and pronounced of nose. So the poem, in all its flourishing virginal inspiration, came to the prefect's attention and the prefect immediately demanded to see its audacious author. Peter was summoned and the meeting lasted two hours, two hours in which they spoke of nothing but the contents of the poem. Another hour was required for Peter's father to explain why the poem had been written, and two more hours for the prefect to explain the terrible evil that it contained, an evil that had to be punished, punished severely.

A great student of the Bible's literary exegesis, the prefect could not believe that such a young head could harbour such categorically diabolical ideas, ideas that could easily spark a revolution of unpredictable consequences. So he went through the poem line by line, a poem that on the surface seemed so inoffensive, or at best made modest allusions to risqué ideas, and he uncovered the treacherous intentions that lurked at the bottom of the author's soul. There was much beard-scratching, for it beggared belief that a stripling like Ngambo could conceive of such manifestly devilish concepts. 'Do you understand what this poem and its ideas could lead to?' demanded the prefect. The boy made no reply and those who knew of the affair assumed his silence was a way of admitting that the prefect had unravelled the thread of his argument and that the reprimand was therefore justified. Or it could be that young Ngambo assumed guilt to raise his own sense of importance. Such things happen with those who aspire to greatness. Whatever it was, there were serious consequences, devastating consequences.

At this point Peter Ngambo interrupted his narrative, saying, 'I will go on to tell more of my father's story and the reasons why I am here, but only after another brother has had the chance to tell his story.'

There was a pause as people digested what Peter had said so far, and then another resident spoke: 'I am happy to pick up where Peter left off and tell of why I am here, far away from my country and my people, though I will not mention anyone or anywhere by name. And when I say I am far away from my people, I do not mean that you are not my people also, that you have not helped me and that we cannot become one big family.'

'Amen, brother,' said a man who must have been a born-again Christian according to the new sources, as preached in many an African city after liberation from the colonial yoke.

'Please do tell us your story,' added someone else. 'But before you get started, I'd like to arrange an *acoté* with you, Peter, if I may. Not now, so as not to hold up the other stories, but soon.'

'An *acoté* about what, brother?' asked Peter. 'Please specify, otherwise I will forget.'

'About what you said earlier, what gets read out on the radio day and night. About the state of mind of black people. It's no small thing to hear someone say that in a place like this.'

'OK, fine,' said Peter. 'We can talk about it whenever you like.'

'Thank you, friend, but not now. On with the story-telling.'

'Thank you,' said the man who'd offered to tell his story next. 'I lived in my *quata* and every day I made the same journey to the mouth of the river looking for work. A man would sometimes show up there in an old wagon and unload a huge pile of hides that needed cleaning. We never asked where the hides came from, nor even gave much thought as to whether the animals they'd once belonged to even existed in our country. All we knew was that we had to take them into the river, scrape off any remaining flesh and scrub them clean. After a while, I decided this was not the job for me: why should I, Peter, for I too am called Peter, although I also go by the name of Darb, get up every day and go and wait for a man to maybe show up, a man who claimed not to be a hunter, but who had piles of hides that needed cleaning. All in all, I only did it two or three times, when there was hardly anyone else there and I was among those selected. The man made us unload the hides, and they stank worse than you can imagine, and then we set about cleaning them. To do so you had to strip down and plunge into the river up to your waist. When I say strip down, I mean down to your pants. At least that's what I did, although some people did strip totally naked.'

'This is a very strange job, brother, if you don't mind me saying,' said someone from under their blanket.

'Let me tell the story!' Peter Darb said, rather excitably. 'This was no ordinary job. The stench of the hides, the fact that none of us knew what animals the skins came from, and also that when you went nude into the water tiny river fishes would be attracted and come to nibble your toes – all these things made it a strange job indeed. And if tiny fishes came, then bigger fishes might come too and peck at something else . . . I don't know if our sisters are yet sleeping.'

'Don't worry, brother, if they're not, they'll play dumb. It's a good story, carry on.'

'And I haven't even started yet!' said Darb, clearly encouraged. 'So, you stripped off and you plunged into the water and the blood and the flesh remains from the hides attracted fishes, big and small ones. Some went for your feet, maybe just for fun, but who was to say they wouldn't go for the other thing? Anyway, it was an awful job.'

'But brother, you said you left your pants on, no?'

'That's right.'

'So, assuming those fishes had come for that other thing and not the flesh from the hides, they'd have had to take your pants off first, and done so without you noticing and jumping out of the water, no?'

'Look, brother, there are women present and I don't really want to go into the precise details. All I'm saying is that the job was unpleasant and dangerous, so dangerous that after doing it three or four times, I never went back again. I would take a different route when I left home of a morning and go and see if there was any work at the old beer factory, where the Chinese unloaded their wares and sometimes needed a hand. So anyway, I lived in my *quata* in a house with a zinc roof and wooden panel walls, and across from my house was another house whose owner I never saw. Sometimes I heard a radio that must have been his, but he either kept himself hidden or hardly spent any time there. I thought I'd eventually see him when he opened the back or bedroom window, but he never did, or if he did, I didn't notice. What I will say, though, is that just looking at the house you could tell the invisible man had money, for the house was firmly built and had raised foundations. Opposite his house were several other houses, houses like mine, owned by people I did see but had very little to do with, and in one of those houses was a little girl, or a baby, and whenever something bothered her she screamed her head off. It was actually quite amazing that so small a creature could make such a noise, as if she was enraged. And in the same house there was another little girl, who was old enough to walk and who would go out into the narrow passageway between the invisible man's house and mine. Or maybe it was the same girl, I never did find out.'

'This is getting interesting,' someone said. 'Carry on, brother.'

'I was at home one day doing something, I don't remember what, fanning myself because of the heat probably, when that curious little girl came up to my door going *ta tata*, which was her way of talking. There was nothing of interest in my house for her, so I half-opened the door and shooed her away, *Go on, back to your own house*. Whether she was the one who was always crying or not, I don't know, maybe there were two strange little girls in that house, but in any case, although she didn't yet know how to talk, I assumed she'd understood me for she went away, back to her own house or off to explore somewhere else. But the visits started to become regular and every time she'd come to the door with her *ta tata*, I'd do the same thing, tell her to go away. Until one day, after I'd told her to go back to her own house, I peeked through a gap in the louvres in my bedroom window, to make sure she was leaving, and what I saw was amazing: truly extraordinary. To recap, I'm in my house, let's say I'm cooking, or fanning myself, or sewing up my trousers, whatever, I hear a *ta tata*, which was like her way of saying, *Hi, Anyone home?* She was a girl who'd learned to walk but couldn't yet talk, and she also, if it was the same girl, cried her head off whenever something bothered her, cried like a grown-up. So, I hear her coming, but I don't want any visitors and I'm not friends with her mother or father, though I did know them, so I open the door and gesture with my hands for her to go away, *Go on, back to your own house*. But that day, after she turns away and goes back round the corner, because like I said, she liked to go in the passageway between my house and the one in front, the invisible man's house, I close the door and go and look through a gap in the louvres of my bedroom window, and in the exact same place where the girl should have been, I see an old woman, a lot older than the little girl's mother even, with a scarf tied over her head. In other words, instead of the little girl, I see an old lady, a woman I've never seen before in my life, calmly walking back down the path.'

'Unbelievable!' someone exclaimed.

'Are you sure you weren't mistaken?' asked someone else.

'I'm going to repeat the story, so there can be no room for doubt. The girl came to my door, but I didn't want her visiting me, so I sent her away, back to her own house. She turned the corner and, from inside the house, I looked out to check she'd gone – I didn't go outside, take her by the hand and lead her away, no. But exactly where that little girl should have been, there was an old woman instead, an old woman with a headscarf covering her hair. This happened not once, but twice, and I don't smoke or drink, I know what I saw: a little girl came to the door, *ta tata*, but when she turned her back and thought I wasn't looking, she turned into an old lady, and she walked calmly away, so that anyone watching would have thought she'd just been to visit me.'

'Let me sit up in order to hear you better, brother. The girl turned into an old lady, a total stranger. She didn't say anything to you, no?'

'She didn't see me, she didn't know I was watching, I doubt she ever knew I'd discovered her secret. Once I'd assured myself that my eyes weren't failing me and that I hadn't got mad, I decided to leave the *quata* and in fact leave the country. That's why I'm here, so far away from home.'

'Brother Peter,' said the man who'd sat up to hear better, 'Where to start? I don't think anyone here can say what you did or didn't see, but your story does raise a number of questions. You're saying that on the way back to her own house the old lady turned back into a little girl again and carried on with her *ta tata*, no? Now was her house close to yours? You don't have to answer if you don't want to.'

'Look, brothers, I've told you the story as I experienced it. You may have your doubts, and every man is free to think whatever he likes, but it's not right to call me a liar.'

'No one's actually calling you a liar,' said another resident who'd also sat up to better digest the story. 'That girl, *tata tata, ta,* came to your door, but you didn't want her to come in. *Off you go, there are no toys here, go on, on your way, I don't want you pissing yourself on my doorstep*. So you sent her on her way and you immediately went back inside your house. Now, she was just a little girl, so she obeyed you and she went away, but because you were afraid of her, or because you didn't want the responsibility of having a little girl in your house or on your property, you followed her with your eyes, whereupon she actually turned into an old woman, only to then turn back into a little girl. So what we need to know is whether there was an old woman who looked like that who lived in the little girl's house. Did you recognise the old woman or was she a total stranger? Because what this actually boils down to, brother, is the distance between your house and the girl's house.'

'I don't want to say much more about it, and anyway, I've never thought the distance between the girl's house and my house was of any importance.'

'Know what, brother? I believe you,' said another resident, 'I believe your story, I don't know why, but I do.'

By now several residents had sat up and they all had something to say.

'Me, I'm the curious type, if such a thing happened to me, I'd follow that girl until I saw exactly how she transformed herself and how she converted back to normal.'

'You have spoken well, but remember, it's not actually your story,' said the man who thought it boiled down to a matter of distance. 'Do you think the same thing could have happened to Peter Ngambo? He probably lived in a district where newspapers came to the door every day and neighbours discussed the latest goings-on over cups of tea. Anyone wanting to turn themselves into a little girl there would have had to do so in front of everyone, or else gone to the bathroom so that no one could see.'

'Don't change the story, oh. It was a little girl who turned into an old lady, not the other way round.'

'But that's my point. Our brother has been looking at this the wrong way round: he actually should have begun by thinking of a woman who lived nearby who might have wanted to visit him. I say this because in my experience it's easier for a woman to turn into a little girl than for a little girl to turn into a woman.'

'Ah, this one will solve the mystery of the chicken and the egg next!'

'It's no joke. If we go on considering the story as being about a little girl, we'll never get to the bottom of it. I just don't actually think a little girl would have the expertise to perform such a wondrous feat. An adult woman on the other hand, well that's a different matter. But brother – what did you say your name was?'

'Darb.'

'You see? Darb is a great name for a story like this. Anyway, what I was saying was that brother Darb had his own issues to deal with, he couldn't actually just drop everything and follow a person just because they turned into a little girl and then back into an old woman again. Besides, in the moment between brother Darb seeing her turn into a woman and him getting out the door to unravel the mystery, she'd have had time to turn herself back to normal again, assuming, that is, she didn't want to be discovered. No, the thing is we tend to think all eyes see the same things, but that's not in fact the case. Furthermore, if you have to worry about finding someone to pay you to clean dirty hides, you don't have time to play detective. The whites aren't actually so dumb that they pay people to go around investigating any old thing. If brother Darb had focused his attention too heavily on this matter, he'd have died of hunger, because he'd have been too busy detecting to go out and find work. Especially if he lived in a neighbourhood where witchcraft was rife.'

'You've spoken a great truth,' said the born-again Christian, 'but I'd still like to know how that little girl would have responded to a good smack, because I'm convinced she was the same child as the one who cried all the time. She knew her life's secrets, brother, it's not your fault that you did not. God bless you.'

11

Sirens were heard down below. It could have been an ambulance; maybe someone was hurt: maybe a policeman was hurt and being taken to hospital. Or it could have been the start of a raid; maybe the residence was about to be purged. For the residence, despite its grandiose name, was really just a cave. That's right, Peter's story and the story of the little girl who turned into an old lady were recounted in a cave, one of the many caves on Mount Gurugu.

Everyone on the mountain came from the heart of Africa, had a past like Peter Ngambo and a brilliant future that awaited them in Europe. They were divided into groups defined by language, for they generally either spoke French or English, although there was a subgroup of people who spoke the languages of Senegal, because they were from Senegal, or had come via Senegal, as quite a number of people had.

Different groups were allocated different caves, although there was mingling and overspill when the camp filled up. They slept on cardboard boxes or on dry leaves, a lucky few under old blankets donated by the

Spanish Red Cross. When they had the will, and when the elements and the environment allowed, they warmed the cave by making a bonfire at its entrance, although they cooked outside. Whenever providence provided a candle, they placed it on a shelf in the rock and curled up beneath its glow, wearing all the clothes they owned.

'I would like to continue my story,' said Peter Ngambo, 'the story of how I ended up in the residence.'

Peter took up where he'd left off and said that his father had been summoned to another meeting with the prefect as soon as the first meeting had ended. A friar was present for the second meeting, a friar of lower rank but of the same order as the prefect. The prefect needed a witness and a second opinion, in order to confirm the seriousness of the offence and the exemplariness of the punishment.

All this happened without anybody knowing the full story, for the fact that Peter's father had glossed the poem wasn't discovered until much later. The gloss was kept secret, the story's unknown element, for although the poem was widely distributed among pupils and the lycée community, the existence, never mind the content, of Peter's father's gloss, which explained the profound thinking behind its creation, wasn't revealed until long after everything had been decided and the punishment imposed, a punishment befitting of such a brazen act of devilment. Indeed it was firmly believed that there was no gloss, that the recriminations were based solely on the superior reading of such a man of letters as the prefect, whose erudition was beyond question and whose interpretation of the matter represented the ultimate truth. So when rumour emerged of the existence of a gloss, it was dismissed as conspiracy theory. Nothing more was said about the matter until the gloss was leaked and finally began to circulate.

Its emergence marked a new chapter in the saga, a chapter in which the gloss became the central focus. At this point the sceptics were forced to renounce their scepticism, or they learned to live with the truth and found a space in the corner of their brain to let the story in, the story of a young student who became a poet and caused a furore in his city's elite education centre. The time had come to find out once and for all what that young bard in the thrall of his muses had meant. In summary, and ignoring the more obscure aspects that will only confuse our story, what the young Ngambo's gloss said was this: Charon, a boatman placed in the imprecise time and geography of ancient myths, is invited, with a degree of insistence, to bring his boat over and go on a journey of discovery to find a certain important centre of femininity. That was the gloss of the first verse and it was at this juncture that the prefect became very serious when interrogating Peter's father, for this important centre was clearly supposed to be a concrete place in the bodily geography of women, and furthermore, duly stimulated – note the young poet's audacity! – it would cause the thousands of virgins inhabiting Islamic paradise to wail in ecstasy. Having acquired this supreme piece of self-knowledge, they would inevitably rise up and confront their little

God, the eunuch heathen, which was why the prefect found the young man's words intolerable. Do you know what would happen if the more zealous followers of the faith you allude to were to learn of what you've written? Can you appreciate what the repercussions would be for our community? More trivial matters than this have seen war break out between previously friendly peoples; much blood has been spilled and many lives ruined over less. The prefect wished to make it quite clear that the boy's insolence merited the strictest of penalties.

'Do you not understand the implications of your words?' the prefect priest demanded of the still very young father of Peter Ngambo.

The young man said nothing and so it was taken as given that he would accept whatever punishment was imposed on him. Indeed, how many people in the world have the wherewithal not to accept whatever punishment is imposed on them? Thus Peter's father's education came to an end. He had insinuated, through the medium of a Conceptist poem, that if the virgins inhabiting Mohammed's heaven were to discover a very sensitive part of their female anatomy, there would be revolution, and this was unforgivable in the eyes of the prefect: first and foremost, it was a crime against religion, even if that religion was fundamentally flawed, and furthermore it was dangerously reckless, for God alone knew where Mohammed's followers kept their hatchets. Such heresy, if transferred to the Catholic faith, would have to be punished, in other words, the poem was blasphemy, never mind the fact that it was aimed at the enemy religion and an unrepentant heathen eunuch manifestly beyond all salvation, as said in Deuteronomy. Blasphemy had to be punished, because he who blasphemed against another religion might very well do so against his own.

At this point Peter Ngambo paused again in his narrative. 'I will continue my father's story only after another brother has had the chance to speak.'

There were a few appreciative nods and sighs, and then another young man sat up and cleared his throat.

'Without wishing to diminish the importance of the story we've just been listening to,' the young man said, 'I'd like to return to the other Peter's story, brother Darb's, which I listened to with great curiosity and no little surprise, indeed astonishment, for it is indeed a small world.'

'Why do you say that, brother . . . ?'

'My name is Alex, Alex Babangida.'

'Welcome, Alex. You wouldn't happen to be from Nigeria, eh?'

'Don't be so quick to link him to the dictator, brother, let him express himself first.'

'That's right, it's not fair to jump to conclusions. Go on, brother Alex, explain yourself: Why are you called Babangida?'

'And I'm the one accused of linking him to the dictator, oh!'

'Will everyone just shut up! It's Alex's turn, so let him speak. Go on, Alex, please, tell us why you were so astonished by brother Darb's story.'

'Well, by the sounds of things I must have lived not fifty yards from brother Darb's house. We're from the same *quata* and yet look where we finally meet!'

'You're saying we were neighbours?' asked Darb.

'That's right,' said Alex.

'But how can you claim this without stating the obvious?' someone else interceded. 'You're saying you're fellow countrymen, no?

'I think so,' said Alex. 'But I swear, I'd never seen brother Darb before I came here.'

'It's not surprising you never saw brother Darb if brother Darb never left his house for fear of being seen by his tatata girlfriend,' said another resident, sniggering. 'It's perfectly normal that this has happened, and you're both most welcome here. Maybe we'll get to celebrate a wedding in this residence yet!'

'What are you talking about, a wedding? Where have got that idea from, eh? You're inventing a story no one has told.'

'I speak of a wedding because there are two neighbours here who've never seen one another before, but if they had met, they might have become love rivals, competing for the affections of the tatata girl.'

Someone burst out laughing. 'This one has very funny ideas.'

'Funny, eh? Anyone who starts out as a little girl and turns into an old lady will have an intermediary stage when she's a young woman, right? So, imagine that young woman, her hair nicely done up, her buttocks firm in those tight trousers young women like to wear these days, and she goes to Darb's house asking for Alex. Now, I bet the price of our entire palace that Darb would say he'd never heard of his neighbour and ask if she wasn't in fact mistaken: Are you sure you're looking for Alex and not Darb?'

The man who'd been laughing was now in hysterics. 'You're saying the girl didn't even know who she was looking for? Ah, this one has a great imagination.'

'Why don't we actually just let Alex tell his story?'

'Yes, do go on, Alex,' said the man who'd spoken of a wedding. 'But feel free to use any of my suggestions. You could say you were the nephew of the old woman the tatata girl turned into, for example.'

'Go on, brother Alex Babangida, tell us your story,' the man in hysterics said with a splutter.

'Thank you, I will, although with all these interruptions, I've almost forgotten it. But yes, I lived in the same neighbourhood as Darb, and it's possible we might have seen one another by chance, without us realising it. I might even have seen his girlfriend, the tatata girl, or the woman she turned into after brother Darb rejected her, but I was never fortunate enough to witness the intermediate stage, when the pretty young woman went to Darb's house asking for me,' said Alex, allowing himself a chuckle. 'So anyway, according to what brother Darb said, I must have lived across from his house, with the house of the girl-woman somewhere in between. The neighbourhood had narrow alleyways and a fair few trees, so it wasn't that easy for people to get to know each other. And as there were few opportunities in that town for people like me and Darb, we constantly had to leave the neighbourhood to earn our crust. On my way home, I often went to the little girl's house, for they ran a grocer's store there and that's where I bought kerosene and things to eat. And it's things to eat I wish to speak of, for I left my land with the distinct impression that someone in my *quata* ate money, that someone being the owner of the grocer's store in the little girl's house.'

'Ah, the plot thickens! Tell us about him eating money.'

'Yes, let me explain. You would go there and order whatever, a litre of kerosene for example, *Hi, I'd like some kerosene*, and they'd give it to you in a glass or plastic bottle, and then you had to go up to a window to pay and you'd see a wealthy man sitting at a table. And I swear, every single time I went up to that window to pay for whatever I'd ordered, a tin of tomatoes or a litre of kerosene or whatever, I saw him feasting on the very thing I was about to pay him with.'

'But he wasn't actually eating the money, brother!'

'No, but that's the impression I got, because you handed over your money and you showed him what items you'd got and he worked out what you owed him and then he gave you your change, if there was any. And he did the whole operation with the same hands he ate his food with.'

'Didn't you just say this man was wealthy?'

'Yes, what of it?'

'Well, didn't he eat with a knife and fork, eh? That's what wealthy men do.'

'No, he ate with his hands, and so every time you bought something there, you left with the image stuck in your head of a fat man handling money and licking his fingers. He would put your money away, and if he needed to give you change he'd find a lower-value note or some coins or whatever and give them to you, and then he went back to his eating, all as if nothing had happened, as if nothing had just passed through his hands.'

'Ah, but he was very trusting of his neighbours.'

'Or very scornful of them.'

'Scornful? Why scornful, eh?'

'Because he actually didn't care that people saw him handling everyone else's money, licking his fingers and then eating.'

'So why not just come right out and call him a dirty pig, eh?'

'Let me finish the story, we'll do the press conference afterwards,' said Alex. 'So, I was just a poor neighbour of that wealthy man, but his behaviour caught my attention, and having heard what brother Darb said about there being a little girl in that house who could turn herself into a woman, I'm now convinced that what they used to say about that man was true. Brother Darb, would you say that man might have been a foreigner?'

'He could have been. I didn't see him often enough to say one way or the other.'

'Ah, this one never bought things in the grocer's so as not to run into his girlfriend,' someone else said, laughing.

'I rarely shopped there, it's true, but that's because I did my shopping before I got home.'

'It's very strange that we never met before, brother Darb,' said Alex, 'because I also cleaned animal hides for a while, for the man who ate money in fact.'

'Hang on a minute,' said another voice. 'You're actually saying the owner of the grocery store was the same man who gave out work down by the river?'

'You're right!' said Darb. 'He was.'

'Well, after you've finished this story you'd better give us some convincing reasons as to why you two actually never met, when not only were you neighbours but colleagues besides.'

'Me, I know why,' someone else said. 'It's obvious, Darb did the job in his underpants, because he didn't want the little fish pecking him on the . . . Are the women asleep? But Alex did the job totally nude. And so now comes the real story, because why did some men do the job nude and others do it wearing their underpants?'

'Yes, why was that?' asked someone else.

'Maybe Peter Darb didn't have the same measurements as Alex Babangida!'

'The same measurements of what?'

'Not everyone is brave enough to reveal their secrets, oh!' the man said with a guffaw. 'But no, what I truly mean is that those who worked in their underpants probably didn't look at those who were naked, or maybe they all worked so hard they looked only at the animal skins, and that is why they didn't recognise each another in the neighbourhood. What do the protagonists themselves say?'

'I say you're all very funny,' Alex laughed. 'But you're also helping to remind me of things I'd forgotten about from back then, so let me go on: there was the man who ate money, a man who thought nothing of putting his hands in his mouth after he'd handled those banknotes and coins.'

'But maybe this only actually happened the one or two times you saw it.'

'Why do you say that, eh?'

'Well, according to what you said, that man was wealthy, he wouldn't have been out looking for work all day, so actually he'd have eaten before you. You went there to buy things to eat or cook, and you'd have been doing so an hour or so after he'd already eaten.'

'Well, I don't really think that's it, although it may well be true that we ate, or I ate, I don't know about brother Darb, after that man had already eaten. But that wasn't what I found strange about him, it was that he didn't care about the dirtiness of the money.'

'What makes a man rich cannot be bad for him!' exclaimed someone, prompting more laughter.

'I'm glad I've brought a little cheer to the residence tonight, but it didn't seem funny to me at the time. Let me explain: from what was said about that man, he was a foreigner and he liked to emphasise his foreignness. Indeed I now recall that he used to pay us in euros.'

'In euros?'

'Yes, in euros. Did he not pay you for cleaning the hides in euros, brother Darb?'

'Oh, I can't remember.'

'Well, I do, and if I'm here now, it's because of the two or three euros I earned cleaning those hides, maybe it was a sign. Anyway, I was told he was a foreigner and that he used to be high up in Idi Amin's regime.'

'Amin Dada the dictator?' someone asked with furrowed brow.

'The very same,' said Alex.

'Goodness, and then after Amin he worked for the Nigerian dictatorship, eh?'

'I don't know about that, but believe me, I've got nothing to do with Babangida the dictator, we have the same name, but that's just a coincidence. So anyway, that man was high up in Amin's regime, and when Milton Obote went after Amin, for it's more likely that's what happened than the other way round, Amin's allies took off, and that's how that foreign man ended up in our *quata*. They say he escaped with a lot of money and weapons taken from the regime he'd served.'

'So he paid you in euros stolen from the Ugandan treasury?'

'Impossible!'

'Why impossible, eh?'

'Because euros didn't even exist back then! Or if one or two did, Amin certainly wouldn't have had any.'

'Let me finish the story, although I'd like to make it quite clear that he may have been rich, but he paid us a pittance. Anyway, what they said about that man was this: he served Amin, perpetrating countless atrocities, which is why he knew Amin's hiding places and was able to escape when his boss made a run for it. He crossed borders at will, greasing palms until he reached Nigeria, where he stopped and set up camp in Yankari Park. Using all the influence he'd accumulated under the dictator, he managed two things: firstly, he made sure nothing bad was ever traced to him; secondly, he got a job as a Yankari Park warden. That didn't happen right away, it took him some time, but as everyone knows, if you can grease the palms of the decision-makers, you'll get what you want eventually. So, he settled down in the nature park and as he'd arrived armed to the hilt, he soon came to rule over the area.'

'Do you mean to tell us he controlled the park using his personal arsenal?'

'I don't mean to tell you anything, but I was told he worked there, and I was also told that he was powerful enough to decide what went on in the areas under his jurisdiction as a park warden, even that he may have overstepped the boundaries sometimes.'

'What about the euros, eh? What about the hides?'

'Wait and let me finish the story. As park warden, that man who'd fled Kampala had the authority to shoot down any animal and do as he pleased with the meat and hides. Quite literally as he pleased, because it's said he was a tremendous glutton, something he'd learned from his boss, Amin, who ate everything, and ate for two or three.'

'OK, so he was a glutton and he ate the meat of the animals in that park, there's nothing so very strange about that. What about the euros, eh?'

'I'm coming to that. It's said he converted his section of the park into private property and began to organise clandestine hunting safaris. The people who took part in these secret safaris paid him in euros, which is why he had euros to pay us for cleaning the hides, though like I said, he didn't pay us many of them.'

'You have spoken well, brother, now it makes sense! Now finally we believe you, and what a great man he was, no? He's a foreigner, he drives to a new country in a 4x4 packed with weapons, his pockets and suitcases stuffed full of stolen money; he greases the palms of those in power, secures a section of Yankari Park for himself and basically becomes lord of the manor. He hunts animals and, having come from a regime of renowned gluttons, he swells his belly and exploits a few fellows cleaning hides, no? Was there any meat to buy in your neighbourhood?'

'I don't know,' said Darb.

'There might have been at the store, the house shop I mean, but I never asked,' said Alex.

'Well, he was a great man all right. See how an African big man gets rich? He organises illegal hunts, the whites pay him vast quantities of euros and he tosses a few crumbs to anyone prepared to clean the skins from his bounty, no? He probably even used the same weapons he'd commandeered in his own country to shoot the animals with. What a great man, no?'

'Great indeed,' said a man who was propped up against the residence wall. 'I ask your kind permission to act as griot, a calling I apparently inherited from my father before I had to leave him and my home because there was nothing to eat. I will tell of that another day, and I also ask that you ignore the fact that I cannot stand up straight, for that too is another story. I, son of Manfu, son of Bayadé, son of Cumyor, son of Manfaré, hailing from the south-west and the north-east, will now perform the story of a great African's downfall, an African who was a colonel major under Chief Amin. Amin became exceedingly powerful, so powerful he even humiliated the Queen of England, expelled the shameless Hindu usurers and was hoisted upon shoulders like the King of Kings he was and always would be. But he erred and his errors were seized upon by his envious enemies and his mighty entourage of lieutenant generals and colonel majors was disbanded, *vrum!, trat, trat, craak!, bum!, Tac tac tac tac creek!* Several days passed and then, *Hallo, I am a Ugandan colonel major and I am venturing abroad, because the houses are on fire down there and enemies are on my trail. Here's a little something for the weekend, for I know times are hard.* And then *flip flip flip*, the dollars leap from his pocket and land in the pockets of the guards at the border crossing. Then *waaaaaa!* Everything goes calm, nobody saw a thing, *Please pass, Sir, go in peace, Good morning, Sir, and Welcome.* Then *craak!* He halted his 4x4 and he put his luggage down and because he was rich and knew his country's secrets, he showed off his potent weaponry and those who ruled the roost in his new habitat were quickly persuaded of his tremendous power and might. *Hey, colonel, nice weaponry, you be in charge of this area and look after the animals. But watch out for the whites, they love stealing ivory. Really? Yes, really, they're crazy about it. Right, at your orders, I'll keep my eyes peeled.* He kept them peeled, peeled as wide as the sky itself, until he could see for miles around. He saw everything, as if he were the all-seeing eye, and into that beady great eye came elephants, rhinoceros, antelopes and any other beast within his reach. As you know, he was armed to the teeth, and he had bountiful ammunition, so no one could constrain him. He settled comfortably into his new position, his new house, his new wife, his new children, and he sat down at his new table and *flop flop flop*, he filled his belly with zebras, rhinoceros, elephants, crocodiles, antelopes and rats. He made people humbly call him Sir and he ate absolutely everything, just like Amin had done, until he grew to be eight feet tall, eight feet of courage and might. Sir's stomach grew into a giant globe and if your nose went anywhere near that enormous belly it got a potent whiff of all the kilos of meat he'd eaten, practically without sharing any of it with anybody. His neighbours didn't even know he had thousands of kilos of meat at his personal disposal every single day. Very few people had the good fortune to ever see that magnificent belly, bulging beneath his foreign tits. Did you have the good fortune, brother Darb?'

'No, brother, I did not,' said Darb trying not to laugh.

'And what about you, brother Alex, did you get to see your neighbour's magnificent belly?' the griot asked.

'I can't imagine how I could have, no.'

'Well, if you'd peered under the table you'd have seen his shiny round stomach packed tight with crocodile meat, although nobody ever knew for sure whether there even were crocodiles in Yankari Park, and so, *I want to buy some salt please mister, OK, give me 50 in notes*, you hand it over, *flip, Here's your change,* and off you go on your way and then you look under the table and you see the stomach, bulbous and magnificent, glinting from the giant turtle he's just devoured, and all that meat made Sir strong, and all those illicit hunts left him with mountains of hides, so many that piled high one on top of the other they were nine feet tall and comprised a huge variety of animal species. With all those skins, and with Amin's madness swelling his head, because he'd been a loyal servant to Amin, he ordered hundreds of drums made and he formed a great army of drummers that *pom pom pom, bum, pom porom pom pom, bum* marched from the park through the jungle and all the way to Victoria Falls, where – '

'Stop!' someone cried.

'What? What's with the interruption?'

'I see where you're going with this, friend. Why do African stories always have to have unhappy endings?' that someone persisted.

'Who told you how the story ends? For all you know they might all live happily ever after,' said the griot, the man who claimed to be Manfu's son.

'Hundreds of drummers march out of the jungle and reach Victoria Falls . . . It's hardly going to end well, is it? I mean, given "Sir" and his backstory, the poor drummers don't really stand a chance.'

'Are you trying to finish off my story for me, brother? Because now I'm confused, are you a griot? Was your father a griot?'

'How about we finish it off together?'

'I just didn't realise your father was a storyteller, that's all. And if he was, why have you kept so quiet until now?'

'Why do you say "my father"? Could my uncle or grandfather not have been a storyteller, or even still be one? Could it not simply be me who's the storyteller? Is it customary in your culture to speak of someone else's father when you've never met them?'

'No, it is not. I didn't mean any offence, brother, I was just taken aback by the way you interrupted me. May I go on telling the story?'

'Yes, brother, finish off the story,' someone else said.

'Of course, friend, finish your story,' the interrupter added. 'But let me share with you a saying from my village: Don't rush to judge the quality of another man's teeth, for he may end up with your whole mouth.'

'And what's that supposed to mean, eh?'

'That maybe you're talking to the only person here who can make sure your story, and the stories of your fellow residents, will cross this sea and be told on the other shore.'

'In that case, I'll shut up and continue only if expressly asked to do so,' the griot said, clasping his hands together as if asking to be forgiven.

'I've given you my blessing, friend, please finish your story.'

'OK, I will continue, but let's light a candle first. In my tradition, a story should not come to an end in the dark.'

'I don't know if there are any matches left. We shouldn't have let the fire go out, we've become slack, the story really ought to end before a roaring fire, no?'

'We didn't have much firewood, we were too tired to gather more. And if we've become slack, it's because these stories have helped us to relax,' someone said.

'I will be bold,' the griot said, 'and finish the story anyway, the story as conceived in Sir General Amin's head. Dressed in their uniformed finery and banging their thousands of drums, the soldiers approached Victoria – '

'Wait, wait,' that someone with the saying said, interrupting again. 'Wouldn't it be more fitting if Sir's army met its demise at the source of the River Nile? I say this because General Amin was from Uganda, a country that's no stranger to waterfalls. Each to their own and a logical conclusion, wouldn't you say?'

'May everyone here be witness to the fact that this brother is saying I don't know the geography of my own continent.'

'Your own continent? Well, that's something we might discuss another time, friend. But for now, please carry on, I just thought it would have been appropriate for the story to come full circle.'

'If this story were yours, you'd be free to end it according to your own science. But it's not, and besides, you'll surely agree that the mad magnitude of the man with nine feet of animal hides is best conveyed if the story matches his greatness, so I'll carry on. That man ate all kinds of meat imaginable, his stomach grew huge and round, though you couldn't see it, you couldn't tell he had such a pronounced and prominent belly. He hunted so endlessly that he managed to accumulate nine feet of animal hides and he built hundreds of drums from their skins and he formed an army with dozens, nay, hundreds of drummers. When his land called out to him, and because the madness in his head had started pouring out of his ears, he ordered his army to march to wherever his grease-addled brain commanded, and so they reached the Victoria Falls of the River Zambezi, and without so much as stripping down, they jumped off, every last one of them, drums and uniformed finery and all. But before they were swallowed by the waters below, three hundred feet down, every African story ever told was preserved for posterity in the rumble and echo of their drums, and that's how the story of the crocodile-devouring glutton ends.'

'Bravo!' someone said, frantically applauding.

'Bravo indeed,' another person said.

'This one is a fine griot, oh,' said someone else.

III

The candle was put out for the night. Alex Babangida, Peter Darb, the griot, Peter Ngambo and all the other inhabitants of the residence covered up their heads, one eye poking out from underneath their blankets. That they had blankets at all was only thanks to the efficient efforts of a charity based in a village in the foothills of the mountain, a village that was in fact more of a town, and which flew the Spanish flag, although it was in Morocco.

Before their dreams could fly them to promised lands, their minds drifted back to the thunder of the drums and the men marching in Amin's underling's army. They'd launched themselves into the void, leaping out over a waterfall and into a river that would take them to the sea, the back door to cherished Europe. Or not even the back door, more like a back yard on the other side of the street, facing away from Europe, meaning their bodies would be buried in accordance with Mother Africa's customs, if indeed their bodies were ever found. Anyone looking for metaphors and paradoxes would be able to open their books and say: Ah, yes, they were heading north, but the Zambezi brought them here, strapped to hundreds of drums made for a glutton escaping prison, a prison built on the orders of his master but intended for others, thousands of others who'd thought themselves his compatriots. Because Amin, it's worth reiterating, ate for three, indeed he was even so bold as to vouch for the taste of his enemies' flesh, and he fornicated until his lust was utterly satiated, robbing pretty young maidens of their virginities and leaving them with nothing but their own misfortune to lament. Girls from the city of Jinja were brought in droves to the nine-foot ogre's bed, and the English gentlemen who witnessed these acts of outrageous barbarity believed them to be African customs. They believed that it was African to shoot dissidents, that it was inherently African to stick a rod up a political prisoner's backside and leave him to die a slow and painful death, indeed so desperate were they to believe these African things that they thought nothing of bowing their heads to allow the poles of the indomitable Conqueror of the British Empire's throne to rest upon their shoulders. Yes, they carried him aloft, thus giving credence to his claims of having triumphed over his enemies, the evil forces that wished him ill. Amin and his full nine feet, which in reality were but six and a few inches, thus ushered in an era in which African civilians were obliged to leave their homelands and go and live elsewhere.

That Amin's name would one day feature in bedtime stories told around the campfire on Mount Gurugu was a macabre form of recognition for such a vicious man. But such was the nature of the storytelling at the residence.

'I will finish my story,' declared Peter Ngambo.

'Ah, your story is deep, brother.'

'You said it. His father spoke French and wanted to be a poet, and that's when things took a turn for the worse. Now I'm not learned enough to understand the poem, but it shocked the perfect.'

'The prefect, brother.'

'Whatever, one poem was all it took for his son to be condemned to a life of nomading. This story is profound, brother. A single poem!'

'Not any old poem, though, eh?'

'Come on, brother. A white man be judging a black man. We all know how that story goes . . . '

'Ah, this one speaks well. A white man was doing the judging, there was only ever going to be one loser, and it wasn't going to be the perfect.'

'The prefect, brother.'

'Know what I think, eh? I think anyone who calls himself perfect is no ordinary person. Even if he'd been judging another white fellow, he'd always have won, I mean, who can defeat a perfect?'

Not Peter's father. He didn't defeat the prefect and he was expelled from the lycée for reasons that would weigh heavily against him. After being expelled, he started to become more conscious of the society he lived in. That's right, he opened his eyes to the world and he realised that those who didn't live in his *yard* spent every day of their lives in zinc huts. He realised that they pissed in the bush or up against crumbling walls, even around the back of their own homes, homes without caretakers or watchmen. That young man discovered that in the city he lived in most boys his age left home first thing in the morning to go out and find work, venturing anywhere they might be lucky enough to get picked out of a line or put on a waiting list. From one day to the next, Peter's father discovered that those who did not live in a house like his had no running water and had to wash or answer nature's call out in the street. He discovered that most people had no decent clothes and that many of them even wore rags and went about barefoot, and that they survived on whatever meagre earnings they made selling fried food from a tray they hawked around town all day. He saw that lots of people had no interest at all in reading newspapers and wouldn't even stop to hear what a man in a tie might be saying on TV, regardless of whether that man was white or black and despite the fact that he evidently led a good life. In other words, Peter's father, who read French and drank tea and liked to take his time about it, found out what country he lived in.

Peter's father went on to discover that a lot of people who went around barefoot and had no interest in what well-dressed men or women, black or white, with nice smiles and even nicer teeth, had to say on TV, were interested in, indeed were fascinated by, anything that had to do with the national football league. Moreover, he found out that football matters in England or Spain were of profound interest to those who lived outside walled compounds, outside the civilised world of tea and daily newspapers. In other words, whether José Mourinho would leave Real Madrid to go to Chelsea, whether he'd secretly spoken to CR7 to persuade him to do likewise, whether Sir Alex Ferguson had insinuated that he maybe might not be in charge of Manchester United for very much longer, even that Emmanuel Adebayor had said nothing at all; these things were considered headline news and provoked heated debate: Who would take the baton from the illustrious Sir Alex? How would Arsène Wenger react to becoming the doyen of the Premier League? When would the true nature of The Special One finally be revealed, bigmouth show-off or pantomime villain? Peter's father saw how hawkers would put their trays of doughnuts down on a pile of bricks and flies could feast with impunity for many minutes, indeed hours, if the game on TV involved two well-known teams. He saw how everyone would stop what they were doing if a shop selling TVs took a chance on security and showed a football match to advertise its wares. Yes, Peter's father, who was still just a schoolboy, saw how children and adults who were oblivious to practically everything snapped to attention whenever football surfaced.

When Peter Ngambo's father opened his eyes and realised he lived in a country very different to the one he'd thought he lived in, he decided to start a family. But not immediately, first he had to face up to the reality of his new life and make sense of his having been expelled from school: it's not easy to deal with the knowledge that your own head is capable of thinking up ideas that might spark a revolution. Look, lad, we're very sorry, and you were even quite a promising student, but we've zero tolerance when it comes to certain things, so you're excluded from all classes. However, we've decided to give you a job in the lycée garden. That was when he became an adult, the moment he decided to start a family. If he hadn't written a poem about eunuchs he'd have gone on being the Ngambo who woke up in a nice house every day and read newspapers. In other words, his true self was perhaps the man he never became, for working as a gardener was not going to allow him to carry on living in the neighbourhood he'd grown up in, nor any kind of neighbourhood where newspapers were delivered for that matter. So Peter's father performed caretaker duties in the garden of a school he'd been excluded from on account of a Conceptist poem deemed too explicit. Or on account of him having had the temerity to gloss it, may God help and protect us, the prefect must have thought, for that school was run by priests with firm and fixed ideas about matters of faith and they had no qualms about abandoning the boy to the city's mean streets.

While performing his duties as a gardener, chief sweeper of leaves, the expelled child became an adult, with adult needs to fulfil. He met a woman, the woman who would become Peter's mother, and Peter was born, the young man whose story this is. They got on with their lives; nothing changed, and yet everything had: Peter's father had grown up expecting to become a man of a certain standing and yet there he was, the gardener in a school that was supposed to have been his ticket to the good life, a school that he left every day to enter the harsh reality of life as lived by his fellow countrymen, a life devoid of poetry.

With his story told, Peter lay back and made himself comfortable on the cardboard boxes that served as his bed. He did not seek approval in the faces of the other residents, nor any other sign that they had enjoyed his story, for he'd no need to: he knew he'd spoken the truth.

'I ask your kind permission to tell my story,' another resident now said, 'and I ask your kind permission that I may remain lying while I tell it, for as the saying goes, if it's not broke, don't fix it.'

'I can't think of a single thing that's not broke around here.'

'What I mean is, I'm comfortable lying as I am. But anyway, I would like to speak of why I left my neighbourhood, what set me out on this path, for when I was listening to the stories of brothers Darb and Alex, I almost started to think I was from the same neighbourhood as them.'

'Don't tell us the tatata girl visited you too, eh? Maybe we'll finally find out who she shacked up with,' someone said, drawing laughter from the other residents.

'No, we weren't really from the same neighbourhood. I suppose what I mean is that you find some things everywhere. I grew up and the house we lived in became small, so I moved to a different neighbourhood. I got a job working for a carpenter and rented a house owned by his sister. I don't remember how much she charged me, and if I don't remember, it can't have been very much. But I do remember that I lived there because of my boss. I won't go into the details of the job, for that would delay the story.'

'But you already said you were a carpenter, no?'

'Yes, but I'd rather leave it at that; I think it's enough to simply state the profession.'

'Then we respect your wishes, brother.'

'The house was semi-detached and made of cement and had one bedroom and a lounge, both of them tiny. At the back there was a door that opened onto a yard where there was a hole in the ground, meaning I didn't have to leave the premises to do my private business.'

'The lap of luxury!'

'Everything would have been fine, never mind that a hole in the ground is really just a hole in the ground and not a bathroom, if it hadn't been for the fact that the house belonged to the sister of my boss.'

'Don't tell me: she came through the back gate, your face was all covered in soapsuds and she took you by surprise, eh?' said someone, prompting more laughter.

'Be patient. That wasn't it, but there was a back gate that opened onto the street and she would sometimes come in through there. She came to check on the animals she kept in one corner of the yard, specifically a duck and two chickens. The duck mostly sat in the corner while the chickens jumped about on a chest, or a coffin, that was propped up against the wall and covered in cloth sacks.'

'Hang on a minute, brother, a coffin is not actually the same thing as a chest. I thought you said you were a carpenter! What did your boss really do?'

'Honestly, it doesn't matter, and if I were to explain everything, it would be a very long story. So anyway, I didn't pay much rent and so I couldn't very well object to my boss's sister making use of her own yard, not even when she started leaving the animals there overnight. But that's when the problems started. I was brought up in a culture of respect and good manners, and so I could not continue to live in that house.'

'Your story is just another version of the tatata girl, only in your case the woman had lost the ability to transform into a little girl, gone past being a young woman and turned into a middle-aged housewife mother, oh!'

The man who'd talked of soapsuds let out a chuckle. 'This one is funny!'

'No, no, it wasn't that. I carried on living there and working for the carpenter. I'd get home, and before doing anything else, like cooking or whatever, I'd take a shower. As I said, the bathroom, or what passed for a bathroom, was outside and so I had to strip off and pour a bucket of water over my head right there in the yard, in front of the animals.'

'The animals?'

'A duck and two chickens.'

'Oh yeah. And so . . . ?'

'Yes, brother, so . . . ?'

'So, that's it. I wasn't used to bathing naked in front of anyone.'

'Brilliant!'

'That's it? What a story, brother!'

'Ha, ha, ha!' The man who'd mentioned soapsuds now couldn't contain himself.

'Do you mean you were afraid the owner would actually come back while you were naked, or are you truly saying . . . '

'Don't laugh, brother, I wasn't comfortable being naked in front of those animals. Because they didn't turn around, they stood right there in front of me, I swear, it was like they were watching me.'

'This one is too funny,' roared the man who'd called the boss's sister a middle-aged housewife.

'Well I don't see what's funny about it! Chickens and ducks have eyes, they must know when a man's naked. If they'd closed their eyes or looked the other way, then fine, but I wasn't accustomed to being watched.'

Almost everyone was laughing now.

'What did you say your name was, eh, brother?'

'I don't believe I did state my name. Are you telling me you'd happily undress in front of domestic animals? Are you saying you'd be totally fine with that?'

'Ah, brother, we're just trying to understand your story. Come on, tell us your name.'

'Mangu.'

'And brother Mangu, you honestly felt like those two chickens and a duck were watching you?'

'My brothers, please don't make me out to be strange. Would you honestly have undressed in the same circumstances?'

'Seeing the effect it's had on you, hell no!' said a voice at the back, producing more laughter.

'Brother Mangu, maybe you should actually try to explain what you were afraid of. What made you ashamed to go naked before the fowl?'

'Why do you now refer to them as fowl, eh?' said Mangu crossly. 'You are deliberately trying to belittle the matter by calling them fowl!'

'I called them fowl because they actually were two chickens and a duck! They weren't people.'

'But I wasn't accustomed to it! Some days I managed to shower before they were brought to the yard, but other times they were already there when I got home from work. And they stood before me, watching me. I put up with it for a time and I tried to get used to it, but I couldn't, so I waited to get paid at the end of the month and then I took off. I walked far and wide seeking a new start, and my steps led me here. I've made it sound brief, but it was a long journey.'

'Congratulations, Mangu, you have gone well and you have spoken well, it's a great story. I don't think there's anything strange about it, but I will ask you one thing: What if it hadn't been fowl, what if it had been camels, for example, eh? Would you have been happy to shower in front of camels?'

'Or parrots?' said the man who'd mentioned the housewife. 'That would be worse, because parrots can talk. They'd have flown from house to house telling everyone what they'd seen . . . Ah, now I understand your story. Ha, ha, ha!'

'Bravo, brother Mangu, bravo,' someone cut in above the laughter. 'If something like that had happened to me, I don't think I'd have had the courage to share it. So I take my hat off to you, brother, bravo. You've shown your greatness.'

PART TWO

I

Dawn broke over Gurugu, pouring light into the residence and over the sleeping beauties stretched out on their folded cardboard. What joy the sun awoke in them, for it brought warmth, as if the cave suddenly had heating. But the jealous trees soon pounced to steal the sun's rays and so the residents reluctantly got out from under their blankets, if they had them.

There was to be a football tournament on the mountain that day. All the Gurugu inhabitants had a special place in their hearts for a favourite idol, someone who represented their immediate futures, and for the most part these idols were footballers: Didier Drogba, Michael Essien, Seydou Keita, Uche Okechukwu, Yaya Touré, Samuel Okunowo, and the leader of them all, Samuel Eto'o. There were many budding or frustrated footballers on the mountain and Samuel Eto'o was foremost in all their thoughts. Eto'o was from Cameroon, but on the mountain he'd become the spiritual leader of all of Africa, the patron saint of all black people on European soil. For the majority of those on Gurugu, Eto'o was an inspiration and beacon, even for those who intended to triumph in a field other than football. That's right, triumph. Do whatever or do everything, but do so triumphantly. Triumph might mean a phone call home, or a letter sent from a European address.

So the Gurugu inhabitants played football every day, in casual kickabouts and in fully fledged tournaments: it didn't matter, so long as the ball kept rolling. Why did the ball have to keep rolling? Why were new arrivals instructed to immediately present themselves to the captain of their group and sign up to a team? Well, for a start, it wasn't healthy to spend all day staring at the city below. Too much time focused on the same one thing could have painful consequences, including stiff necks and failing eyesight. Yes, failing eyesight, because by spending so many hours on the mountain, and the hours on Gurugu were many and long, there was the risk of all manner of vices being born among them. It would have been a very different story if the mountain had been theirs, if it had been donated to them by one of the King of Morocco's daughters, for then they might have turned it into a plantation and grown things to eat and to sell. People would have come from across Africa, from everywhere north of the Zambezi, from Cameroon, Mali, Nigeria and Niger, from Mauritania, Senegal and Guinea, even from Morocco, those dissatisfied at being disregarded subjects, and they would have founded the People's Republic of Samuel Eto'o on Mount Gurugu. Then they would have demonstrated the great knowledge and agrarian expertise of their respective lands by cultivating favourite plants: from the hard Gurugu soil there would have sprung sweet potatoes, new potatoes, yucas and even rice. And once they were up and running they would have started to get serious and the land would have yielded fish to accompany the harvested potatoes. That's right, such would have been the optimism and energy of the good folk of the People's Republic of Samuel Eto'o that they would have believed themselves capable of cultivating fish and they'd have built swimming pools on the mountain to farm fish this big and this tasty, all because of the circus of them having been made citizens. Fish, which the Cameroonians would have grilled and accompanied with bumper crops of yuca, fish with thick spines and delicious bones that the Malians would have licked with delight, fish with couscous, for the cleverest of the new citizens would have even built special cubicles with the right microclimatic conditions to grow wheat in. It would have been their own land, to do with as they pleased, and so they would have acquired cattle and put them out to pasture, and imagine how their mouths would have watered as they prepared a bowl of couscous to set on the table beside a succulent pot of lamb stew. There would have been so much to do that the ball would have only rolled once or twice a week, for there would have been hundreds of tasks to perform in order to make the People's Republic of Samuel Eto'o an independent and self-sufficient nation. And once it had become one, and once appetites had been satisfied and thirsts quenched, they would have sought justice.

But the mountain wasn't theirs and so the ball had to keep rolling. Why did the ball have to keep rolling when there was barely any land on the mountain fit for playing football? Because conditions on Gurugu were not as most people from the Zambezi north imagined them to be. You can spend all hours of the day dressed in shorts in Doaula and two items of clothing suffice in Bamako, but the uncomfortable truth is that on Mount Gurugu the elements are rather less accommodating. In a sense, the Gurugu inhabitants had already reached Europe, for although they weren't the sort of temperatures that would have troubled the average European, if you'd just come from, say, San Pedro, Senegal, it was very, very cold. Not cold enough to draw television crews perhaps, but if you were camping on the mountain because life had closed in on you elsewhere, your teeth chattered, especially at certain times of the year. The Gurugu inhabitants had barely any clothing and some didn't even have the roof of a cave or a tent over their heads. Plus they had to prevent their gaze, if not their thoughts, from lingering too long on the town below, and so they sought solace in Samuel Eto'o's calling. There was nothing else for it, they could either burn down the mountain making endless campfires or they could run around after a ball and let the warm embrace of exercise bring a few hours comfort and respite. Run after a ball or any round thing, for often what passed for a ball on Gurugu would have made their footballing idols laugh. But anything roughly round and fairly light sufficed on Gurugu, for it was better to have something to chase after than to sit around trembling in the cold. You had to keep moving, you had to keep going, you had to play, even if you'd never played football in your life before, because if you didn't, you suffered, you ached, you saddened, and through bouts of shivering fits, even though the cold wasn't all that cold, you began to lose heart and think that someone had better give you a reason to be hopeful, and soon.

'Good morning, Peter. We need to eat breakfast, it's match day, the semi-finals.'

'Good morning, Alex, yes, we need to eat breakfast.'

'You're not interested in the match?'

'What makes you say that?'

'You said "yes, we need to eat breakfast", but you didn't mention the match.'

'Well, you can't have seen me walking recently. Haven't you noticed my limp?'

'No, brother, sorry. What's the matter?'

Peter sat up in his bed and shrugged his shoulders, as if to say it ought to be obvious.

'Okay, well, we'd still better tell the captain.'

'And what about breakfast, eh?'

'Well, you can't play on an empty stomach, but if you're not playing . . . '

It was a universal truth that you couldn't play football on an empty stomach, but there were other truths on the mountain, important truths to do with why the ball had to keep rolling and why so many people had limps.

'Anyway, come on, let's help with the lists.'

The residents compiled two lists. For the first list, the captain thought of everyone who was available to play football and he soon reached eleven names. A few feet away, others worked on a second list, one which required even more careful consideration than usual, for it was match day and football was an important business. As they worked on the list, the sun climbed up the horizon and the breeze brought fresh air: a new day had dawned, a new day that would bring new demands. Soon the second list was complete. It was a shopping list of everything the men and women of black Africa needed to survive in the residence. It was a mental list, for there was no pen and paper.

Two residents set off with the shopping list in their heads. As they made their way down the hill, one of them started thinking about all the food there was on the African continent, a train of thought that had begun while helping compile the shopping list. He'd thought: 'Imagine if we had an elephant.' That's right, an elephant, just the one, one elephant for the five hundred or so men and women gathered on Mount Gurugu. 'Imagine if the park warden who'd escaped from Idi Amin's Praetorian Guard sent us just one elephant, we'd have enough meat to feed ourselves for months on end:

'"Hello, Sir, you don't know me, but I've come to Yankari Park especially to see you, for I must tell you about the situation further north, a fair distance from here. There are some five hundred of us, black Africans all, and we just want to live, you know? We just want to live, but living is a serious business in Africa, for it's often very hard and lots of people barely manage it. We're in a place called Gurugu where we're divided into language groups, principally English speakers and French speakers, although there are other groups too, because there are sometimes lots of people from a particular place and they speak their own language. Anyway, we basically spend the day playing football, for reasons I won't go into, but in order to play football, often with a ball no bigger than an orange, we need to eat. Do you understand me, Sir? Eat or *manger*, according to whichever history the whites chose for you. If Sir could just see to it that an elephant, just one single elephant, could reach us, the meat would last us for months. We would carve the elephant up and set aside the non-edible parts, such as the contents of its digestive tracts, although we wouldn't throw them away, for in a place with so little, everything has its worth. Do you understand what I'm saying, Sir? We'd find a way to chop the beast up into pieces and then we'd take some of the meat to sell on the streets of Melilla."

'"And the two tusks," Sir would say, "don't forget about the tusks, they'd fetch a pretty packet."

'"Of course, Sir, you're right, that's the first thing we'd do. We'd sell the tusks and then we'd sell some of the meat."

'"Okay, son, but your plan is flawed somehow," Sir would say. "Melilla is a European city, you can't just wander the streets hawking raw chunks of elephant meat. As for the tusks, forget it, ivory poaching is strictly forbidden in Europe, at least it is if you get caught, what you do secretly is another matter. But your story interests me, so do carry on, just don't think I haven't somehow noticed these flaws."

'"If you send an elephant to Gurugu, Sir, we'll cut it in two, and we'll sell the tusks and some of the meat secretly. With the money we get we'll buy rice, onions, olive oil, garlic, cooking pots, drinking cups, tomatoes, potatoes, vinegar, kerosene, buckets, milk, condensed milk, drinking cups, seasoning, flour, butter, chickpeas, lentils, couscous, oats, chicken, rabbit, raisins, oranges, apples, lamb, sweets, bananas, flour and cheese. We'll go back to the mountain with all our groceries and we'll cook the delicious leftover elephant meat . . . "

'"Yes, what will you do with all the leftover meat? Because you can feed an army on an elephant."

'"I'd rather there was no talk of arms, Sir, for the arms that pour into Africa are a major cause of the problem we find ourselves in."

'"I said an army, I didn't mention arms specifically."

'"Please let me finish my story before you start talking of arms, Sir, if that's what interests you. Returning to the leftover meat, we wouldn't buy a giant fridge to store it in, no, because we'd need the money to continue our journey."

'"Onwards and upwards, eh?"

'"Look, Sir, I've doubtless forgotten to include other items on the list, but I really must mention salt. Lots of salt. Because, after cooking a giant pot of food for everyone, or each group could cook its own pot and its preferred accompaniments, we'd cure the leftover meat using the salt. We'd gather dry branches fallen from the mountain trees, and take a few green branches too, and we'd make a bed to lay the meat on and underneath the bed we'd make a fire, to dry the meat out, to smoke it and cure it, so that it could be eaten for many months to come."

'"And what would you do with the elephant's innards?"

'"The innards are the tastiest parts, so they'd be awarded to the winners of the football tournament."

'"And what about the brain? Would that not somehow go to you, because I understand you're the captain of one of the teams?"

'"I hadn't thought about the brain, and no, Sir, I'm not a captain. Why did you think I was?"

'"Because you speak more than one language. Anyway, I'm sorry to pop the bad news, but don't you know elephant meat is haram?"

'"Elephant meat isn't haram, Sir."

'"How do you know? Are you somehow a Muslim?"

'"I'm not Muslim, but in my travels along rivers I've gathered experience."

'"Well, I don't mean to contradict you, but can you imagine the environmental scandal an elephant sacrifice on a civilised mountain would entail? All that blood everywhere, the stench from the innards and the contents of the elephant's digestive tracts, never mind the billows of smoke you'd make curing the leftover meat . . . This cocktail of ingredients would turn Mount Goo . . . Gru . . . "

'"Gurugu, Sir."

'"Would turn Mount Gurugu into Dante's inferno. Do you know who first told me about Dante's inferno?"

'"No, Sir, I don't."

'"The English advisor to His Excellency Idi Amin Dada, Conqueror of the British Empire."

'"But he's dead, Sir."

'"Who? His Excellency's English advisor?"

'"No, Idi Amin."

'"Well, if he died, he died with his titles, but actually he's not dead. Anyway, firstly, elephant meat is haram, secondly, I somehow don't think the Moroccan police would tolerate you turning the mountain into some barbaric horror scene. One dead pachyderm and the whole camp would be razed for good."

'"Are you sure, Sir?"

'"Very sure, though it pains me to say it, because elephant meat is indeed a fine delicacy. Even if it is haram, and anyway, such luxuries are not really for the likes of you, a simple black who somehow decides to abandon his country because he wants to go to Europe and marry a white girl."'

Such were the thoughts of one of the men as the two envoys made their way down the hill to seek food in Farkhana.

'What are you so busy thinking about, brother?' the other envoy suddenly asked.

'Idi Amin.'

'Amin? The dictator? Why think about him, eh? Anyway, there's something I need to tell you, brother, something I need to tell you in confidence.'

'Go ahead, friend.'

'There's a certain item women use at a particular time. We have to find out what it's called, because one of our sisters is bleeding and needs it.'

'You mean she's got her period?'

'She's bleeding, brother, I don't think I need say more.'

'But is she bleeding or menstruating? It's not necessarily the same thing. How serious is it?'

'It's serious enough for us to have been asked to add the item to the shopping list, brother. We have to find out what they call it in their language down there and add it to the list.'

'We can add it to the list, it costs nothing to add something to the list. Whether we can get hold of it or not, that's another matter, because we certainly can't afford it.'

'I know, brother, and it's going to be awkward, asking strangers for something so intimate, which we don't know the word for.'

'It's not our fault, friend, we're not in our own land.'

'I know, brother, but the whole situation, it's enough to make you want to go mad, because then – '

'There's nothing to be gained by us losing our heads.'

'No? If we were mad, it would be a whole lot easier to ask strangers for something we don't know the name of, something we have to ask for because blood is spouting out of our sisters, we don't even know why and yet – '

'What do you mean we don't know why? We know why blood comes out of our sisters, or is there more to this than you're letting on?'

'Please stop interrupting me, brother.'

'Come on, don't get cross with me, friend. Communal living isn't easy.'

'But you're acting like you're oblivious to what's going on and that's not right, brother, that's no way for a responsible person to behave. We have to go into a corner shop or a supermarket and find out the name of the product we need, a product that we really shouldn't have to ask for, because it shouldn't be lacking in the first place, and because women shouldn't have to leave their villages and their work in the fields to seek a new life elsewhere, because – '

'But the reality is – '

'Stop interrupting me!'

'But something has obviously happened! You're clearly upset about something and unless you tell me what it is, I don't see how this can be a successful trip. Come on, let's sit down on that rock over there and you can tell me what the matter is, aside from the ridiculous fact that we live in a cave and call it a residence so as not to die of shame before illness or a Moroccan bullet gets us first.'

'You want to know what's upsetting me, eh, brother? Does it seem reasonable to you that we have to go around begging for an item we've never used and don't know the name of, eh? We don't speak Berber, we don't even speak Spanish. So what do we say, eh? We can hardly act it out! We can beg for something to eat, the pain of hunger has been universal since the twelfth century BC, but times have changed for women, even if we are back to living in caves.'

'I'm sensing there's been an accident of some sort, am I right?'

The other man lowered his head as tears welled in his eyes. But they had to push on and they had to prepare themselves to overcome their shame and beg for food, in an alien language besides. That's why one of the envoys wished he were mad, for madness would have taken away his inhibitions. You're an adult, you're black, you live in no-man's land on a mountain watched over by armed police who don't like you being there. Hunger is eating a hole in you, several holes in fact, and the trees on the mountain bear no fruit, not even bitter fruit. You have to head for the lights of civilisation, the nearest town. Look, good citizens, as you know, we live up there, because you won't open your doors to us and the immigration centre is full to bursting. We're not going to die of hunger just to make life easy for the chief of police, so we've come to beg, to beg you for something to eat.

'What do you want?'

'*Aliments*, please, *la nourriture*.'

'Look, all I can give you are a few onions and potatoes left over from yesterday.'

'*Merci, merci* very much . . . And now how do we ask for the other thing, eh, brother?'

'What?' said the woman. 'What's the matter?'

The time had come to ask for the sanitary towels.

'Ah, I wish I were mad,' said the envoy who'd said it before.

'What's the matter with you? I've given you what I can, I don't have any more, the crisis affects us all, you know? This is Morocco, not Sweden or Denmark, or even Germany.'

'No, *Señora,* look, *por favor, ecrito, ecrito.*'

The lady took the scrap of paper and squinted, trying to make out the word written in improvised ink.

'Goodness me! No, *lo siento*, I'm no longer of an age to use them. I don't have any, I'm very sorry. You'll have to go to a supermarket or a corner shop, and good luck to you.'

'*Merci, madame.*'

'May Allah have mercy on you.'

Two potatoes and a few onions. Without all the meat in Yankari Park, even with the army having perished in the Zambezi's waters, two potatoes and a few onions was a very light breakfast for the legions of footballers on Mount Gurugu. The two black men looked at one another. It was never good when envoys came back to the camp so empty-handed. Each group looked after its own affairs, but they shared whatever they got hold of and if there wasn't enough to go around the residence, there'd be nothing to offer anyone else. But it was more than that; it was a statement of sorts: the inhabitants of Farkhana have nothing for the blacks who've invaded their forest.

'If that woman spoke Spanish, she can't have been Muslim, eh, brother? Unless we've totally misunderstood how things work down here.'

'You can't expect to understand them, we're not from here. She is whatever fate determined her to be.'

'But what do we do now, brother? We don't have enough food and we've failed to get hold of the thing the women need. Ah, I wish I would just lose my mind and not have to worry about any of this.'

'Your pride will protect your reason, friend. Come on, we've no choice, we'll carry on asking, we have to survive.'

'But do you think that woman really didn't have what we asked her for?'

'She gave us what she had.'

'But all women use them, don't they, eh?'

'What do you mean by all women?'

'All women, grown-up women with households and children.'

'How old are you exactly?'

'Twenty-two. Why?'

'No reason. Come on, we'll keep on asking.'

They wandered through the streets of Farkhana begging for food and the other thing, something specific, something that was needed to contain the blood spilling from the sisters who'd accompanied them on their adventure. Eventually their rumbling tummies reminded them that you couldn't play football on an empty stomach and that they ought to head back with what little they had. Going back up the mountain was tiring, but the energy it required brought them warmth. When they got back to the camp, they found it unusually quiet. Look, we got this and this, but we couldn't get that, what can we say, they either didn't know what it was or they directed us towards the shops. But the two envoys realised the

Gurugu inhabitants were preoccupied with something else, so they stopped a man who approached them on the path.

'Did something happen while we were away, eh, brother?'

'More like while you were home. Did you get what the women asked for?'

'No. We kept being pointed towards the shops. Why?'

'One of our sisters has fallen ill.'

'I know, brother, but has something else happened, eh?'

'There's been a meeting. Omar Salanga is in our midst.'

The man went on his way, leaving the two envoys to look blankly at one another.

'Who's Omar Salanga?'

'I don't know, but I've heard the name before.'

'Omar? Is that an anglophone or a francophone name, eh, brother?'

'It can't be anglophone, friend, it's a Muslim name. It must be francophone, or Senegalese.'

'Or Ghanaian. I'll go and ask that brother over there,' said the younger envoy, the one who was twenty-two. 'Ah, excuse me brother, have you heard of this Omar Salanga? Where's he from, eh?'

'It doesn't matter where he's from. The important thing is he's here.'

'But why is he so important? Who is he?'

'Ask Aliko.'

'Aliko? Who's he, brother?'

'You don't know Aliko Dangote?'

'I'm new to this forest, brother, I still don't know everyone.'

'You know the guy who goes around in a blue anorak? That's Salanga, Omar Salanga. Aliko you usually see in a red checked shirt, with his hands in his trouser pockets, as if he weren't cold.'

'If he's got his hands in his pockets, then surely he's cold, eh, brother?'

'I meant the checked shirt. It's not enough for the temperatures we get up here.'

'He must drink something to keep him warm then, brother. Or else he's very tough.'

'Tougher than the whites, certainly. But maybe you're right, maybe he drinks too. When did you get here?'

'Two days ago, brother. But don't ask me where I came from. It was via lots of places, but I came in through Algeria. They told me I no longer have a country, that's what they said at the border: you've no country any more, now you're just black.'

'Well, once you get to know your way around, you'll soon learn who Aliko is.'

'Ah, but I want to cross soon, brother, I haven't come all this way to hang about.'

'I know you haven't, brother, but still.'

The two envoys got back to their residence, the cave they'd been assigned to when they first arrived on the mountain. They told the others how they'd fared, the trials and tribulations they'd faced in trying to get something to eat, and how they'd had to dedicate much of their time to seeking something that had proved difficult to get hold of, in fact impossible, something scribbled down on a scrap of paper. Either the people they'd asked hadn't understood or they, the envoys, hadn't asked correctly. Or it could have been that the women they'd asked had all been too mature and no longer needed something to curtail the blood of a monthly discharge.

'We didn't manage to get it,' the younger envoy said. 'And now they need it more than ever.'

'Why now more than ever?' said the older envoy.

'It's a delicate subject, that's what they said at the meeting, because the mountain is like a giant house, but with many ears.'

'So has something serious happened?'

'Let's get the food ready first. We'll talk about it during the match.'

A few onions and two potatoes, plus a lettuce salvaged from a market that had already packed up for the day. Those who'd gone for water returned and the pot was put on to boil. Infusions were prepared, for the mountain was generous in this regard, and then each group did its best to share whatever it had managed to procure. After eating, everyone joined together to spend the rest of the day talking about the future and playing football.

'When we close our eyes at night and blow out the candle in order to ration it, we'd do well to remember that we are the lucky ones, for we live in a palace with a roof over our heads.'

'Okay, brother, I promise not to go mad. But what are we going to do about the women now that we've failed to get what they needed?'

'We'll have to go back down, friend. We'll take one of them with us if necessary, she can explain the situation to a woman down there.'

'Ah, but one of them can't walk, brother, and the other has gone further up the mountain looking for medicinal plant leaves.'

'She can't walk? It must be serious. We have to get her out of here.'

'I know, brother, but if we can't even manage to get hold of a simple item that's commonly used by women everywhere, how likely is it that we'll find someone who'll welcome us into their home and offer her treatment, eh?'

'We'll take her to a hospital.'

'No hospital round here will treat blacks without papers.'

'I know, but we've got to do something. What's the matter with her anyway? There seems to be a lot of mystery surrounding this.'

'Because the mountain is a giant ear, brother. Apparently nobody would say it outright at the meeting, but Aliko's name was on the tip of everyone's tongue.'

'Aliko? Ah, so he's involved in this. Right, come down to the lookout area with me, friend, if the match kicks off while we're gone, the captain can put someone else in our place.'

'Okay, brother, let's go.'

Those who knew the most about the camp and its surrounds were based halfway up the mountain. They were the ones who put out the warning whenever danger approached, danger in the form of the Moroccan police. The alarm sounded and everyone fled, hiding as best they could in the mountain's nooks and crannies, praying to God not to let the rabid Moroccan police find them. I smell blood, I'm going to break your black legs and ankles so you can't walk, maybe you'll even end up dead, and nobody will know, nobody!

The two envoys arrived at the lower part of the camp and explained what had brought them there, that something very bad had happened to two women in their cave.

'Sorry, brothers, but we can't evacuate anybody right now.'

'Why not?'

'The Moroccan police say no one's to go down the hill, no matter what the circumstances.'

'But two of our sisters are sick, one of them is very unwell, and we don't know what to do. And when I say she's very unwell, please, brother, try to understand me.'

'Yeah, we know, we've received word too. But nobody can leave, and besides, it's important we resolve this matter here on the mountain, amongst ourselves. My advice to you is not to get involved. Let us deal with Aliko and Omar, we'll speak to the veterans in the Senegalese group.'

'Why that group particularly, eh?'

'No reason. Because they're impartial. Look, if I mentioned them it's because they speak French and Bambara, which they talk among themselves, and because they have a certain influence over the Guineans and some other folk they share vernaculars with. Besides, the Canary Islands are right in front of their country, they're used to being this close to Europe.'

'And are these the only reasons?'

'Look, brother, down here we judge things differently.'

'Okay, I understand. Thank you.'

'No, thank you. Go well.'

II

From Mount Gurugu, your future was mapped out: you could see where you needed to get to, the path you had to take in order to follow in Samuel Eto'o's footsteps. Samuel Eto'o was so attractive as a role model that many of the men on Gurugu played football in order to keep fit for when Chelsea or Barcelona signed them. They toiled away trying out the dribbles and drills they'd heard Eto'o practised, their president and commander-in-chief. Or if not Eto'o then Messi, or the maestro, Ronaldinho.

There were a number of world-beaters on Gurugu and they played every day, but today there would be a four-nations tournament, so it was especially important they were limbered up and sharp. The four nations were Mali, Senegal, Cameroon and Nigeria. Anyone who came from a country with insufficient numbers to form a full team could be a substitute for whichever of the four nations they chose. In this manner, those from Niger signed up with Mali, Senegal welcomed the Guineans and the Gambians joined Nigeria. Indeed it could easily have been a five-nations tournament if the Burkina Faso contingent had banded together with others from Benin and the Ivory Coast.

Whenever Gambians played against Malians, there was a good deal of banter. It was one of the rare occasions when the inhabitants revealed their flags, if only symbolically.

'You Gambians marry old ladies. We pity you. Marriage should be about having children.'

'That may be so, but I won't take pity from someone who's never seen the sea.'

'Bah, poor old English ladies come over, Allah is great, seeking men their own age, but presently when they find them, they discover they're impotent, too hypnotised by the tide to go and find plant medicines to keep them strong and long-lasting. So the poor English ladies resort to boys young enough to be their own grandchildren, and so the great lie begins.'

'Hey, what great lie, brother? Love knows no age.'

'Love doesn't, but the body does. A cured fish can't get back in the river and start swimming again.'

'Is that a Malian saying? It must be, because it mentions a river and not the sea. But I'll tell you a Gambian saying: the heart is forever young.'

'But the body gets evermore old. It dries up, and once the dryness has reached a certain level, the body can presently no longer bear fruit,' one of the Malians said.

'Hey, do you mention dryness to remind us of the terrible drought devastating your country, despite the fact that His Most Merciful was kind enough to let the Niger River run through it?'

'Bah, and do you mention rivers to remind us that if you removed the Gambia River from your plaything of a country, there'd be nothing left!'

'I'd like to sit you down in a London restaurant and finish this argument properly. But as it is, we'll have to beat you at football instead.'

'Pweeeeeee,' went the sound of a whistle. 'The tournament is suspended.'

'What?' several people cried.

'There was an accident in the night and a woman is very sick.'

'God have mercy.'

'The tournament is suspended. Gather the captains, there's to be a meeting.'

The players dispersed while the captains gathered around the referee. He was a man well-respected by all, for he'd been a referee many years previously, when his country had functioned differently. Something had disturbed the peace on Gurugu and needed to be set right. The captains formed a circle around the referee and waited for him to inform them as to why the tournament had been suspended. Meanwhile, the other inhabitants split up according to their own interests and affinities and started playing football anyway.

'You, you, you and you, against us four. That's the goal; Djibril, you be mister referee. And blow for everything, all right? Just because the ball is not really a ball doesn't mean we shouldn't play the proper rules, although admittedly it's almost impossible to play offside on such a small pitch.'

'So are we playing for offside or not?'

'We are,' said Djibril very seriously.

'But it's impossible to play offside on such a small pitch.'

'Why did you ask then, eh?' said Djibril.

'What? So is there offside or not?'

'Pwee,' shouted Djibril, for he had no whistle. 'The first half is under way!'

He refused to state whether offside would be taken into account or not. On the one hand, it was obviously excessive to insist on observing every last law of the game, but on the other, in an unstable environment overseen only by themselves, it was important that rules be respected, even in a kickabout. In any case, offside was largely irrelevant, the important thing was to keep on moving, to run around until night fell and you could no longer see the ball. You couldn't see the ball, but you could see the lights in the villages below, and although those villages were not in Europe, they had lights, meaning prosperous lives clustered together. Pweee, foul, yellow card. You see this leaf? See what colour it is? That's for you, brother. Next time, you're off. Someone sat down to rest. He'd run around enough to keep himself warm for a while and so he swapped places with Djibril, who'd been sitting on a rock, refereeing with his arms folded across his chest. Football, even football played with a ball the size of an orange, was the principal energy source for Gurugu's Sub-Saharans, with due respect to the sun and apologies to the trees whose branches were burned on grey afternoons.

On Mount Gurugu you ran around to keep warm, but on sunnier days you headed for the mountain spring. There were no bathroom facilities on Gurugu and so personal hygiene was a sensitive subject. When the weather was good, you went to the spring, stripped down as best you could and bathed, and if someone had managed to beg a bottle of shower gel in Beni Ansar or buy a bar of soap with hoarded money, you bathed all the more conscientiously. Either way, you used a tin can to pour water over your head and it was up to you whether you stripped totally naked or not.

Among the mountain inhabitants there were a number of Christians and they'd read the Bible and knew about the woman Adam had found lying beside him when he'd come round after passing out. Should Adam not have made a run for it once he'd recovered from his momentary loss of consciousness? Because Adam, in all his innocence and fear of God, was unaware of the existence of women and so he would have understandably been terrified to waken, rub his eyes and discover a long-haired monster with pointy bits at the breast and a clitoris trained upon him. Or did Eve not have long hair? It's hard to imagine the first woman to walk the earth did so bald!

She would have approached Adam, intimidated him with her breasts and tried to touch him. Or maybe she found the first man's manhood amusing and thought it a toy, grabbed hold of it and shook it like a rattle. Naturally, Adam would have run away horrified, screaming with fear. He would have thought the woman an apparition, an evil spirit come from the nether regions to test him and lead him to perdition, for the Bible clearly states that 'God created the great sea-monsters, and every living creature that moveth'. Adam would have known the earth was full of monsters and assumed this long-haired woman was one of them, indeed she would have been one to him.

Next comes the issue of language, for just as it's hard to believe Eve was bald, it's difficult to imagine Adam and Eve came into the world speaking tongues. Remember the tatata of the little girl who proved not to be a little girl after all? Remember how she was banished from that young man's premises? Well something similar would have happened with Eve, only it would have been more dramatic, for there was the added factor that Adam was naked. Stark naked, without a stitch on him, because in the era the Good Lord had chosen for him, temperatures allowed for that sort of thing.

On Mount Gurugu, men stood under the jet of water that came out from between the rocks and scrubbed themselves down, all the more conscientiously if there was shower gel or soap, although such items weren't shared around amongst all the inhabitants because there were hundreds of them and it wouldn't have gone far. They scrubbed themselves down and they got back under the jet, or scooped their tin cans into the water and tipped them over their heads, and they rinsed the last soap off their bodies and let themselves dry off under God's own sun, because nobody could charge them for that. Once dry, they put their clothes back on, the same clothes as before, the same clothes they'd been wearing for two months or more, the same clothes they'd slept in every night on top of their piece of cardboard, or directly on the bare earth if they weren't lucky enough to have anything to disguise their poverty. The same clothes they'd walked thousands of miles in to get to Gurugu. They put them back on, perhaps wringing out the neck to check for any hidden last drops, for sometimes the sun lasted long enough for them to take off all their clothes and wash them, with soap if there was any. They did this terrified of an unexpected visit by the Moroccan forestry police, imploring the sky to let the king of stars shine bright and return their clothes to a state of dryness before the police discovered their naked black bodies, for it's important to remember that the Moroccan forestry police corps was set up specifically to preside over the black people on Gurugu, as soon as black people realised Gurugu was a strategic place to get some sleep. But if none of this occurred, if the sun didn't shine, if generous souls hadn't donated shower gel and prudent black hands hadn't hoarded coins to buy soap, then they stripped down, they washed quickly and they put the same pants back on, the same T-shirt back on, the same shirt back on, the same socks back on, the same trousers back on and the same whatever they were using as a coat back on. As should be fairly obvious, Gurugu wasn't the sort of place where you might enjoy the simple pleasure of a change of clothes. No. You put the same clothes back on and you put up with the hum of having lived in them for several months in impoverished solitude, but with your desire still intact, without that yet having drained out of you. Pity your cave companions, or fellow bunkers in a tarpaulin tent, if they happened to have a sharp nose.

People played football on Gurugu to keep warm and busy, for the hours were long and football enabled them to lose track of time, but in a different set of circumstances, they'd have read all day and into the night. And in a different reality, a team of African scholars would have come to Gurugu mountain to talk to the inhabitants and to ask them to comment on Peter's father's poem. *Charon, bring hither that boat / we'll away to the lake's end / reach the exact point of femininity*. The African scholars would have doubtless been surprised by what the people on Gurugu had to say on the subject. The first two lines would have been discussed for hours on end, and then there would have been the little matter of what the poet meant by *the exact point of femininity*. Some of the mountain's inhabitants were illiterate, never having had the opportunity to learn to read or write, and they would have had a good deal to ponder when one of the scholars explained who Charon was. It would have given them much food for thought and several among them would have felt inclined to retrace their steps, the hundreds of miles of steps through the desert that led back to their home towns. The story of Charon, an old man with a boat who was paid up front with a coin, would have saddened them a great deal, because it would have made them think of their own journey, and that it didn't deserve to end in tragedy. From the Sahara to the Zambezi, there was surely too much to eat for them to end up at the mercy of a surly, scrawny, temperamental old man. Those first three lines would have forced them to reflect on their own lives and plans.

The scholars didn't come, but the second verse nevertheless gave the Gambians more means to argue with the Malians:

'What do you think the poet meant by the heathen eunuch, hey? I'd say it refers to the despicable custom, practised in your country, I do believe, whereby you must avoid women until your mother decides it's time you got married, and the fact that some men go their whole life without knowing what lies beneath the ten feet of fabric you force your women to wear in your parched and dusty land.'

'Ha, ha, ha,' a Malian laughed. 'You're very funny, but your nervousness betrays you, for the bit about false faithfulness and the eunuch clearly refers to you. Everyone knows no good can come of a young man tying the knot with a woman presently past her expiry date, and here we have the tale of a eunuch loyal to a deposed queen with a dry womb. You speak of our mothers, when yours must weep on your wedding night imagining the sweat you have to work up . . . Well, you know what I mean, I shan't go into the details.'

'Hey, you don't have to go into the details, but tell me, how come you speak English?'

'Bah, I spent two years working on a boat from your country, brother.'

'I thought as much! Two years on a boat hoping to catch the eye of an English lady . . . '

'Come on, please, my culture does not allow me to go with a woman who's presently old enough to be my grandmother. I would rather give blood in a hospital than have it sucked out of me by a grandma.'

'So you're telling me you'd rather die of thirst in the desert than get on a plane and go visit your London in-laws?'

'Do I look like a man with no self-respect?' said the man from Mali. 'I'm not going to Europe to beg, I've got a profession.'

'Hey, are you suggesting we Gambians don't have professions?'

'Bah, professions you may have, women your own age presently you do not. Now I have to go and get water for my group. But before I go, let me say that what goes on in your country is best described in Latin!'

There was much discussion on the mountain following the cancellation of the football tournament, and there was laughter too, nervous, genuine and forced. The Gurugu inhabitants were clearly troubled by something that had happened in their midst, the most obvious consequence being the suspension of the first match. Smaller games went ahead and fended off the cold, but did nothing to temper the unrest. This became evident in the tone and topics of conversation, for although everyone on the mountain knew where everyone else was from, it was considered best practice to keep your nationality secret. The fewer clues you offered the Moroccan forestry police the better, or any other police force for that matter, and so the rule of thumb was that the closer you got to the gates of Europe, the more you disposed of anything linking you to a concrete African country. On Gurugu you revealed your origins only to those you truly trusted, and yet the origin of one African is hardly an unknown quantity to another. That conversation between the Malian and the Gambian could, therefore, be read as playful banter, but it was also a symptom of the simmering tensions. The two men had spoken clearly and at length about their own countries, and this just a few miles from the first flag of the European Union. This was not an incident without precedent, for the Gurugu inhabitants had learned their lessons the hard way, following a curious incident that ended as it did because of an article of faith.

The weight of destiny became too much to bear for some on Gurugu: it was dreadfully cold, the Moroccan police had clamped down on anyone going into the villages to beg and their provisions had run out. Hunger grated. It had come to the attention of some of them that part of the mountain was the natural habitat of the Barbary macaque, and they thought: monkey, meat, food. Their situation was desperate and so they decided they must take matters into their own hands. They went out into the forest, to a section that was some distance away from the camp, and they managed to catch one. How? It's a valid question, because monkeys are not easy to catch. The hunters had a fair amount of luck, it's fair to say, but the only meaningful answer is that hunger, especially hunger suffered collectively by hundreds of men, and a few women too, inspires ingenuity: they caught the monkey thanks to the ingenuity of several among them. They hunted down that monkey and they caught it and then they set about preparing it to be cooked and eaten, to appease their wretched hunger. First, they skinned it. Or half-skinned it, for they were in the middle of doing so when the Moroccan police arrived and caught them red-handed. For a police force as conscientious as the Moroccan forestry police corps, it was no longer a simple matter of a bunch of black Africans occupying a mountain that didn't belong to them, that in fact belonged to Morocco, for they had now killed an animal, and a protected species at that. This was the accusation that weighed most heavily against them, for the Barbary macaque was protected, they'd killed one, and the Moroccan authorities were strict upholders of the law: the consequences would surely be dire.

But in the end they weren't, and it was the very fact that the Moroccan authorities were such strict upholders of the law that saved them. Upholders of Islamic law and firm believers, for the offence went unpunished because of Sura 2, Verse 65 of the Koran: 'Be ye apes, repugnant and hated'. The Barbary macaque may well have been a protected species, but such protection, whether genuine or invented, and no matter how necessary, contravened the official religion of Morocco, a country where the king himself was Commander of the Faithful. There was some debate about whether the macaque was an ape or a monkey and whether it mattered, until it was decided that any beast implied to be repugnant by the Koran simply could not be defended. The hunters were released, but the conscientious Moroccan police still felt it their duty to punish them and so they were summarily beaten, in a secluded spot lest anyone see the police avenging an animal reviled by His Most irrefutably Merciful, the highest authority of all. The monkey hunters eventually returned to the camp, alive and at liberty, but with very visible signs of the repugnance they'd caused and the words of Sura 2, Verse 65 ringing in their ears.

This should have been a cause for celebration, for the hunters had returned with the monkey meat and hunger was rife on the mountain. But there was no such cheer, indeed the poachers were greeted with considerable hostility: many of the Gurugu inhabitants were themselves Muslim and although they felt sorry for their bruised companions, they also thought the police had done right. Such was the sense of unease, word soon spread that the men who'd been caught with their dirty hands in the dirty meat were from Cameroon. Of course, the faithful said, they come from the jungle, they're heathen, such vile deeds are only to be expected. But it was rare for an incident to be accredited to a concrete nationality and it would lead to important lessons being learned.

The Muslim faithful departed and left those of a different persuasion to roast the monkey meat and indulge. The Cameroonians tried to claim, continuing the line of defence they'd adopted with the police, that the animal they'd been caught with was not a monkey, but a rabbit, and that it had been given to them in charity at the Beni Enzar souk. But the Islamists wouldn't buy it, and the whole episode had anyway left them feeling repulsed. Besides, good Muslims that they were, they would surely have known that a rabbit's head is much smaller than a monkey's. And good Muslims they may have been, but the mountain air still informed them of how succulent the barbecued haram meat was as the Christians and atheists enjoyed their feast. *Bon appetit*, they would have said as human beings, but as followers of Mohammed they went hungry.

That the Cameroonians had been singled out generated considerable discontent in the camp, for the most zealous practitioners of Islam continued to claim they'd got their just deserts for having disregarded Verse 65, Sura 2. That's when the veterans from the lower reaches of the Gurugu camp intervened. From that moment on, it was declared that matters of patria would be the private business of individuals and that this was to be observed for the good of everyone. If you had a flag, a recording of the national anthem, a photo of the president, or the president's wife, or Miss wherever you were from, or anything personal and non-transferable, such as an original and genuine passport, you were to keep it hidden and make sure no outside agent ever found it, for it linked you to who you'd once been and could therefore be used against you by the powers that be, powers that would one day rule on your future. Nobody was asked to renounce their own countries, towns, customs, folk songs, militant tendencies, national heroes or anything like that. You were just asked to use discretion, and you were told that if a particular souvenir felt like an amulet to you, then you'd do well to query its efficiency, for such querying would serve you well in the long run. Viewed from a distance, such precautions may seem excessive or even cynical, but not when seen from within. They were merely the logical conclusions reached by one of the veterans, a man who was over forty years old and had known nothing of his village for five years, five years in which he'd not worked, aside for the odd job to ensure his survival.

As has been stated before, no team of professors or learned scholars came to the mountain to discuss the poem or ask the inhabitants about their immediate and non-immediate concerns, but if they had come, they would have talked about profound matters and they would have broken the poem down into a thousand pieces and said very profound things about each and every part, with the African continent as the constant backdrop, leading them to say a thousand more profound things about change as experienced by the good men and women of Africa. Yes, if the scholars had come to Gurugu, they would have had a fruitful time of it and left feeling intellectually nourished. But before they had quite departed, indeed with the bulk of the party having already set off, one of the scholars would have paused and made a passing comment, and that comment would have led to another long debate. For the learned man would have observed all the running around on Gurugu and felt compelled to say something to one of the footballers, and this would have been met with a frown by one of his well-read colleagues.

'You may sneer, professor,' the scholar would have said, 'and it may be true that honourable and erudite men of letters don't talk about football, but I believe it deserves a lot more attention than it gets. I mean intellectual attention, of course, for it certainly gets enough of the other kind.'

'Is the good doctor really saying that footer, an activity as simple as two men chasing after an elastic ball, deserves the attention of the academic community?' his colleague would have replied.

'Firstly, professor, football is much more than two men, or even eleven men, or indeed eleven women, or boys, or girls, chasing after a ball, be it made of elastic, as you said, or any other material. Are you really sure they make footballs out of elastic?'

'Well, if they don't, they should.'

'I'll make a note of that. But back to what I was saying: football is not just a bunch of men chasing after a ball, the classic pejorative description used to trivialise the sport. No, football consists of a formation of men, or sometimes women, endeavouring to get the ball into the opposition's goal while conforming to a set of rules – rules I emphasise, lest complacent intellectuals underestimate the game's complexity.'

'I see you hold footer in extremely high regard.'

'Footer, if that's what you wish to call it, deserves our scientific attention, for there's much more to it than meets the eye. Twenty-first century man, *hominis XXI*, typically dwells in an urban agglomeration of over five million people. He suffers from all the hatred, tedium, neglect, pressure, bitterness and stress one might expect in such a mass of humanity, and if there wasn't somewhere for him to go and scream from time to time, to go and shout insults, cry and generally let off some steam, life would become perilous. It's hard to predict what would happen.'

'But it is possible to predict now, because of football?'

'Football has discredited previous human behaviour theories based on religion, the occult and politics. Researchers and philosophers ought to be mesmerised by a phenomenon that is neither mysterious nor confers power, because for millions of people, there is literally nothing more important than football.'

'I suppose, doctor, that at some point in your discourse you will recognise that football is big business.'

'I will, but first let me say that the difference between football and other sports, for example Formula 1, is that football doesn't use up vital natural resources and contaminate the environment: football is clean, quiet and cheap. With no more than, say, eight hundred footballs, elastic or otherwise, the game could be played everywhere in the world. It does, it's true, eat up a little electricity if played at night under floodlights, but it needn't be, and it does require some nice grass, and that can be expensive to maintain, but that's really only for the big teams. Generally speaking, football is clean and cheap and profitable.'

'Finally he says it!'

'Apologies, professor, a poor choice of word on my part, I did not mean financial profits, I meant that society benefits from football being played.'

'But profits are made. You say it's cheap, but goodness, matches aren't free to go to, stadiums aren't cheap to build!'

'It is indeed true that stadiums are expensive to build, but I would also say that their construction provides work to a lot of people and that once they've been built they last for many years. Furthermore, they are necessary, because you can't very well ask thousands of men to stand on each other's heads, one on top of the other, forming giant columns, in order to watch the spectacle, and it is necessary that the game be played and watched because, and this is my main point, football breaks down society's class structures: football is played by plebeians and venerated by aristocrats; football opens the nobility's palace doors to street urchins and outcasts.'

'That sounds somewhat overblown.'

'Professor, don't mock something so serious. Millions of people live in cities that are physically and mentally overcrowded and if there were nothing to placate them, they'd snap. We'd return to the days of the Roman circus, but with genetically modified elephant-tigers developed in the most sophisticated laboratories on the planet. Men and women imprisoned for who knows what petty crime would be led into the arena and forced to take on the elephant-tigers. We occasionally hear of young lovers somewhere condemned to be whipped or stoned for having had relations before marriage, and there's an international outcry. Now imagine those young lovers being thrown to the elephant-tigers!'

'You mention laboratories, doctor. Maybe you're thinking of doping, so prevalent among our footballers.'

'I will not rise to such provocation. But I will say this: there's no way that a few grams of whatever it may be, some substance you'll be more familiar with than me, can turn someone usually only capable of hoofing the ball, into a player of great talent and flair. Do you really think drugs could have made Thomas Gravesen play like Zinedine Zidane? Turned Marco Materazzi into Andrea Pirlo? You can't possibly believe that even a kilo of chemicals could have helped Fabien Barthez become as good a goalkeeper as Peter Rufai?'

'Can you explain the relationship between football and the occult?' one of the Gurugu inhabitants would have interjected. 'I didn't understand when you mentioned it earlier.'

'It's quite simple, lad. We used to think people behaved in a particular way towards certain things because those things were mysterious or governed by a hidden power.

The idea of a hidden power is very attractive, hence religion and occult sects. But football turns the theory on its head: football fans behave exactly as if devotion will bring them salvation or eternal life, and yet football celebrates its liturgy out in the open. Not even the Pope can compete with football these days.'

'A panacea, dear doctor,' the professor would have said, with a touch of sarcasm.

'A complete sport, dear professor. Football combines the best of athletics, judo, American football and swimming.'

'Care to add any other virtues?' the professor would have said with a snort.

'Certainly I would. Go to a tollbooth on any European motorway, or to a hypermarket, or simply switch on the TV: you won't see them. You won't see them driving their cars, doing their weekly shop or presenting a programme, and if you do, they will be the exceptions that prove the divide-and-rule. I'm sure you know what I'm referring to, professor, for there are millions of people in the world who never study geography, and without studying what lies beyond their immediate surrounds, they never learn that black people exist. But we do, and against all the odds, we are there for all the world to see at any international sporting occasion. It's the only reason millions of people know black people exist. There is no other way: do what you will, you won't be seen. There are fewer of us thus exposed than there might be, for sure, but there are still some, and when you consider that nobody can love what they don't know exists, it's reasonable to say that those few blacks seen chasing after a ball on TV achieve a good deal more than any number of conferences on Africa organised by the world's leading universities.'

'Sorry, sir, I still didn't get what you said about football and the occult,' the Gurugu inhabitant would have asked again.

'And besides – sorry, lad, bear with me – football, as well as perhaps television, is one of very few things that have a positive instructive influence on young folk without meaning to, and I'm talking about fundamental issues. Any European country with a lying demagogue for a leader can talk about integration until the cows come home, without doing anything to make it happen. Yet thanks to football, black children living in Europe have people of their own race to look up to. If it weren't for black footballers being on TV, do you know what black children would say they want to be when they grow up? Not doctors or astronauts or scientists or policemen, for they wouldn't know about them, let alone judges or detectives, and least of all bankers. They wouldn't want to be anything. What do you want to be when you grow up, kid? And silence. They can't know if they've never seen an adult of their own colour doing any job of dignity. You can't expect a child, no matter how humble, to say when I grow up I want to be an agency cleaner at Charles de Gaulle airport. Or when I grow up I want to be a fake-handbag salesman, never mind a razor-wire acrobat or a shipwreck rescuee. These aren't professions. It's football that teaches children that black people get to go on TV, get to be admired and applauded. Perhaps they don't all end up saying they want to be footballers, but they see a brother up there on the screen, someone from their tribe who has triumphed, and he speaks for them all. I don't think it's any exaggeration to say that football is the key to survival for countless black boys. And when I say football, I of course mean footer. Now what was it you wanted to ask me, lad?'

'About the relationship between . . . '

'Ah yes, what I meant was that we used to think that man only lost his reason when it came to serious things, like God, the occult, family, patriotism and sex, when called love, but now we know that he is perfectly capable of losing it for unserious things too, like football.'

'Many thanks, sir.'

'No problem, son.'

'You've offered a rather flimsy apologia for the religion of footer, doctor, although I must say, what you just said to that boy undermined everything that came before it.'

'I have two strata of listeners and I address each in their own way. I could go on for a while yet, but I've said the main things: football is useful, universal, clean and necessary. If Hindus haven't learned to appreciate it yet, well that's their problem, I mean, they wanted to play barefoot . . . '

All this would have been said if the learned scholars had come to the mountain and shown an interest in the black people living on Gurugu, an interest in their immediate and non-immediate concerns. But we all know how it is with Africa, what's hoped for never comes, and so the black people who lived there had to focus their attention on living, in a very harsh environment, doing what they could to survive, doing the only thing available to them: playing football.

III

After the tournament was suspended, everyone was on tenterhooks and everything that went on in the camp reflected the unrest. A Gambian and a Malian reminding one another of the virtues and vices of their respective nations was much ado about nothing compared to what had caused the unease in the first place, and so the tension mounted, until the word 'kill' was heard. Yes, some people believed that an individual, or in fact more than one, had transgressed to such a degree that the community should take justice into its own hands. It was, therefore, a transgression deemed vastly more grievous than the incident involving the hungry Cameroonians and the protected primate, but it similarly risked attracting the attention of the Moroccan authorities, and such a fatal form of retribution would surely give the fearsome Moroccan forestry police carte blanche to do their worst. The situation grew increasingly heated and the fresh water that came from Mother Africa's womb and sprung out into the world on Mount Gurugu was needed to cool many heads.

As the details emerged, it became clear that whatever had happened had much to do with an unsavoury character who went by the name of Salanga. Yes, Omar Salanga. It was said that Salanga had conspired with another Gurugu inhabitant, a man called Aliko Dangote. The curious thing was that many people were acquainted with Aliko, but suddenly they only had bad things to say about him. It was as if the entire camp lacked the energy to abort the plans for punishment now that they'd been set in motion. So who really was Omar Salanga and who was his crony, a man with a name as apparently plain as Aliko Dangote?

The story of who Omar was quickly spread around the camp and although it spread as most African stories do, via word of mouth, those who came from the same place as Omar confirmed that it was true. They had never doubted his existence, they understood he was very much a man of flesh and blood, and they had been taught to be extremely wary of him.

Omar Salanga had lived in a village somewhere and whenever he felt he was overheating, he'd taken a path to a nearby river. There he found women and children washing clothes or bathing, but Omar was too much of a man to share the water, and so he forced the women and children, some of them girls, to get out of the river. That river, at least the stretch that passed close to the village and took his fancy, was to be his and his alone. He took off all his clothes, except for a pair of gumboots, the sort used by armies, for it was said Omar had been a soldier in former times. Then he got into the water.

Those who remember the facts about Omar Salanga, if facts are indeed what they are, recall that everyone knew of him in the village, a village that was maybe not his own but that of his parents, and the women knew that if they went to the river to wash and Omar Salanga showed up, then bad luck, they would have to go unwashed that day. For when Omar stripped off all his clothes, aside from his boots, and got into the water, he would float leisurely back and forth with a cigarette dangling from his lips. His aim, or so the people who saw him concluded, was to disappear inside himself, to remove himself of all earthly concerns. His going back and forth didn't mean that he went from one riverbank to the other, veering around the rocks in the middle, rather that he went up and down the river, as if the business of being at one with himself required that he alternate forays upstream, pushing against the current, with ventures downstream, going with the flow, towards a hypothetical meeting with the sea. And it came to be considered some kind of ritual, because he always did it and he always did it completely free of clothes, but wearing those boots, and always with a drooping cigarette hanging at the edge of his lips. Up and down, as if he'd decided to head to the river's birthplace, only to change his mind on recalling its resting place.

That's what was said about Omar Salanga, and indeed they said more. The manner in which he visited the river didn't overly bother the women, rather it was the way he took so very long about it. Furthermore, they hadn't gone to the river to witness a spectacle and, if the truth of the story be told, what bothered them even more than the simple waste of time was that while banished into the foliage, they had to take great care to protect the moral well-being of the girls who were present, their own daughters for the most part, or those of their neighbours, because that man went about unashamedly naked and he had an unusually large member. So it wasn't so much that he prevented their quick hands from promptly getting the household clothes washed that annoyed them, rather it was the moral threat he posed, especially with so many innocent young girls around. And boys, because in African villages little boys don't mix with adult men until they're of a certain age. So it was a case of don't look, girls, nor you, boys, this is not appropriate viewing for children of your age. Look towards the mountains instead, and do so until that man has had his fill of smoking and bathing, until he puts his clothes back on and goes back into the forest. Yes, what they said about that man was that he liked to take his time in the river, having expelled everyone else from it, women and children, and he only got out when the mood took him. When he did get out, he didn't take the path back to the village, rather he went into the nearby forest to smoke, or to carry on smoking. So another question is what sort of tobacco was he smoking while he went back and forth in the river wearing nothing but a pair of boots? Well, whatever sort it was, he needed to smoke more of it, and so he went into the forest, and later on they learned that it was *banga*, and that he got it from somewhere down by the river. But why didn't he smoke it right there, by the river, where nobody would have bothered him, given that he'd established himself as lord and master of his surrounds? Nobody knew the answer.

So there were two factors to contend with, the first being that Omar forced the women to leave the river, stopping them from performing their tasks, and the second being that he would have contaminated the minds of minors if they'd come face to face with his naked manhood. Such a thing wasn't for little girls' eyes, nor indeed the eyes of sensitive women. A regular user of the river knew right away what was up when she approached the water and saw numerous women with their sons and daughters, and the sons and daughters of others, huddled in the nearby forest, stealing an occasional glance at the river to see whether Omar had yet left, so that washing rituals could be resumed. They stole the occasional glance, but they knew they'd be well aware if he'd departed, for he usually walked right past them as he left, before veering off from the path that everyone else used. His not using the same path as everyone else lent further mystery to the man. But the main thing was that for a good many minutes, and once for over an hour, nobody else was allowed to use the river, a river that should have been for the benefit of everyone. You might have gone to the river to wash yourself, or you might even have been halfway through washing, when Omar came along and curtly barked out his orders. You got out, you took your tub, you collected your soapy clothes and you headed off, away from the river, so as not to expose your eyes to harmful things. And the eyes of others too, of course, other more impressionable eyes. So you moved away, good mother and responsible adult that you were, and you let Omar Salanga go up and down the river, you let him smoke, go up and down, smoke, up and down, smoke, and you tried to ignore his manhood and his lording it over the river, public morality and the river beasts that might nibble his toes if he didn't keep those enormous boots on. And because everyone knew what would happen if the self-appointed king of the river came along, the women started to bring things to eat whenever they went to the river. And when the street hawkers got wind of what was happening with that man and his strange smoking habits, they started going down to the river with their trays of fried and baked wares, for washing clothes is a hungry, thirsty, tiring business. And because that man who took possession of the river did so regularly and in such a leisurely fashion, a small market selling refreshments began to form by the river. Nobody could approach the water while that man was in it, 'nobody' being women and children, so they passed the time snacking on whatever was on offer and within their reach, their monetary reach. The snacking started out as a distraction and turned into a custom, and soon, whenever Omar Salanga was seen heading for the river, a market quickly formed and everyone took it for granted that it would form and be there for as long as that man was in the water, then pack up and go when he got out and went into the forest to smoke *banga*. And that's how Omar Day was born. Or Omar's Market. Omar's Market Day. Omar's Day. Omar's Mini Market.

The people who witnessed and suffered those inconveniences ended up incorporating them into their daily routines and in this manner Omar's Market was established down by the river, on its western bank, far enough from the water's edge to ensure little girls weren't exposed to disturbing sights. It's said Omar himself stopped at the market only once, asking to buy tobacco. Which kind of tobacco? What brand? Did he smoke regular roll-ups while he floated up and down the river, but the forbidden kind under the trees, when the forest filled with acrid fumes? Things would have gone on like this forever, or for as long as that man lived, or perhaps until a stronger man than him came along and made him see the error of his ways, but then something else happened, something that had nothing to do with the market that had been named after him.

There were a number of Christians in that village where people had come to accept Salanga's authority, and they were preparing for an important event in their calendar: the first communion of a number of boys and girls. The boys and girls had passed a series of tests set for them by the minor hierarchy of the local church and their families had been informed that they would soon receive the body of Christ. When the big day came round, the mother of one of the girls rushed out of her house with her daughter in tow, for she planned to give the girl a thorough soak in the river. The girl usually bathed herself before mass or school, but this was a special day and the mother had determined to supervise, the better to make sure she was spotless when she received Christ for the very first time. It would be a proud and transcendental moment and her daughter had to be immaculate.

Such occasions involve a multitude of tasks and you have to plan ahead to get everything done and not be late for the ceremony. So they set out for the river in good time, today's your big day and there mustn't be a speck on you when you enter God's temple, and with nervous tension they fairly scurried along, and they reached the river and there they came upon Omar, as previously described. 'Good Heavens!' the woman exclaimed, in the language she used to speak of matters of God, before adding 'Jesus, Mary and Joseph!' for good measure. Acting quickly, because she knew her daughter's delicate little soul was in danger, she made a shield with her hand and placed it before her daughter's eyes. When a child accompanies an adult along forest paths, the child usually goes on ahead, for no responsible woman wants her little one to get left behind, so it is highly likely that what she wished to avoid had already occurred. 'Oh no,' said the woman, 'what a catastrophe!' All she could do was cover her daughter's eyes to prevent further damage. Now she, as an adult woman, faced quite a dilemma, because there was no time to waste and yet who was she to disturb Omar's leisurely bath? If she'd been as strong as him, or as strong as he was thought to be, because a weakling would surely not have taken such a defiant attitude, weaklings don't have markets named after them, then she would have confronted him and suffered the consequences, demanded that he either put some clothes on or go upstream to bathe. But she wasn't as strong as him, or didn't think she was, and so she didn't confront him, but she also knew nobody would wait for them if they were late for the day's main event. Whoever was in charge might have had a list with the girls' names on and might have done a tally and might have noticed someone was missing and might have held up the ceremony for a few minutes. But they wouldn't have waited very long, allowances couldn't be made for a girl running late because her family hadn't finished sewing the buttons onto her outfit or hadn't finished making her look sufficiently angelic for the most important day of her life. So the woman didn't know what to do, other than make sure her daughter's eyes weren't further stung by the sight of that man's shameless nudity. She knew she had to hurry, so she thought quickly and she approached the river, ignoring the terrible fact that Omar was in it, and she filled her bucket with water, thank goodness she'd brought one, and then focused her energies on giving her daughter a thorough scrub, all the while averting the girl's eyes from the disturbing scene nearby. She had to go into the river a second time to get more water, for this was the girl's first sacrament, it was a unique occasion and she had to be perfectly clean. The woman came back with a second bucket of water and washed her daughter thoroughly and then she dried her down, gave her the special knickers she would wear for the ceremony and a piece of fabric to cover up her chest. They would finish dressing her at home.

They left the river and as soon as they did so the mother was struck by how scandalous the whole affair was. It was outrageous that her daughter should be exposed to such a sight, and when the girl's heart was pure besides, for she'd confessed the previous afternoon in readiness to receive the Lord. The mother began to cry and she cried all the way home, where family members were busy preparing food and setting up for the party. They rushed out when they saw her and they asked what dreadful misfortune had brought tears on such a glorious day.

'My poor girl,' spluttered the girl's mother, 'and today of all days, when she's already confessed.'

The mother's primary concern was the state of her daughter's soul, which had been tarnished by its encounter with Omar Salanga's nudity. The girl's purity had to be recovered in time for the Catholic ceremony that would mark her definitively. A discussion ensued involving the entire family and one or two neighbours, and it was decided that the best thing to do was to take the girl to see the priest again and have him take away the burden of what she'd seen. So that's what they did, and they managed to do it quickly enough for the girl to get to church on time and receive her first communion, freshly confessed and clean of conscience, thus ensuring the Christian ritual would have an everlasting effect. Seeing the unabsolved Omar Salanga in the raw was a sin that would have prohibited her from taking holy communion, and indeed she would have been prevented from doing so had it not been for the priest's intervention.

But that wasn't the end of the affair. That a woman had come back from the river weeping and had furthermore been forced to seek an extra confession for her daughter on the very day of her first communion, was no small thing. Several members of the parish sat up and took notice of what was happening, and they decided something had to be done. What that something would be was left to the parish priest, and he decided to cordially invite the church choir to deal with the matter. The church choir? Well, the girls and boys and young men and women who rehearsed twice a week and provided vocal accompaniment to the celebration of holy mass. They sang along to the music and, as orchestrated by the priest, took the volume up a notch or two whenever the congregation threatened to doze off or began to yawn excessively. Okay, girls and boys, I'd like you to look into a delicate matter whereby a man has been terrorising some of our male parishioners with his outrageous behaviour. Yes, the priest said male, when in fact the terrorised parishioners were female. Did he speak of males instead of females to avoid a scandal?

'Do you want us to use our sweet voices to sing the evil out of him, Father Priest?'

'I appreciate your sense of humour, but unless the situation deteriorates, hopefully a well-recited prayer will be enough to settle the poor man's corrupt heart.'

'If we find him, we'll bring him here for Your Reverence to pray for him.'

'If that's what the heavenly council wants, it will happen of its own accord.'

Was it not remarkable that the church choir was sent out on such a mission? Young boys and girls, and others who were no longer so young for they'd reached the age of desire, were in the full flush of desire in fact, instructed to go into the forest and have a few words with Omar the outlaw, whom they'd probably find as naked as Adam in the Garden of Eden. Was it not possible, indeed likely, that within that choir there would have been friends or relatives of the girl whose honour had been desecrated on the day of her first communion? Would they have cowered before the man or smelled revenge? And what would have happened if, when the eager young choristers tracked down the unrepentant Omar Salanga, they launched into Latin song? For good God, that man, that usurper of the river, that miscreant who lived on society's margins, deserved to feel the full brunt of a hymn sung in Latin, maybe one that went something like this:

Tellus dormit
et liberi in diem faciunt
numquam extinguunt
ne expergisci possint.
Omnia dividit
tragoedia coram
amandum quae.

Et nocte perpetua
ehem vel vera visione
par oram videbo te
mane tempu expergiscendi.

As he floated up and down with a cigarette hanging from his lips, Omar and anyone else in earshot of the river would have been overawed by the Latin echoing from the choir's lips. The words would have pounded his eardrums and he'd have looked at his naked self and felt great shame, for the Latin sung at him would have been so exalted and so solemn that he would have suddenly become acutely aware of his spiritual inadequacies. He would have heard the song loud and clear and he would have understood that *Tellus dormit et liberi* referred to his libertine ways, and that *numquam extinguunt* was a thorough condemnation of his reprehensible lifestyle, a lifestyle headed for disaster, hence the choir's intervention and the *tragoedia coram*. And he most definitively would have recognised *mane tempu expergiscendi* as a terrible reprimand, perhaps even damnation, for a period of time at least.

But African traditions are still strong, in fact all the more so since matters of God started to be pronounced in local tongues, and so it's likely Omar Salanga was admonished in a language more familiar to him than Latin. But we don't know. That expedition struck out into the forest and made for the stretch of river commandeered by the man, but it's not known what they sang when they got there. In other words, although it was public knowledge that the choir was sent to attend to the matter, what they did, or even if they did anything, when they got to the riverbank, has never been properly explained. Did they say anything to Omar that might be classed as a reprimand? Did they even see Omar? It's never been suggested that they didn't, and the subsequent conduct of some of those who took part in the expedition led many people to believe that they must have seen him, but whether they made contact with him is a different matter. The choir never spoke of it and so whether the punitive Christian initiative bore fruit or not remained a mystery. Was the outlaw made to see reason or did he impose his own reprehensible reason on the choir? Nobody knew, and so the story gained a life of its own and quickly turned to legend. What did the members of that girl's parish choir say to Omar Salanga? What did Omar say to the eager young parishioners? Did they see him naked with a roll-up dangling from the edge of his mouth? Did they witness his extravagance in the river, bandying his large manhood about in the altogether? Did they notice the fact that he was naked except for those military gumboots and that he got them wet when he could have easily taken them off to enter the water?

What impression Omar made on the choristers who saw him, if indeed they saw him, never leaked out. Did the girls in the choir see him and that's why nobody wanted to say anything? Could that even have been the reason why some of them joined the expedition in the first place? The facts of the matter, facts that would have enabled future generations to talk of the affair from an informed perspective, were never revealed and so speculation filled the void. Rumour spread and the story became folklore.

The story was embellished with hundreds of details over many years, and with every new detail, Omar's fame grew. It was said that the brave intervention of the choir had driven Omar out of the county, but very few people actually believed this and nobody got very far looking for proof. So conjecture grew, and every time the subject was raised new elements emerged about who Omar was and what might have happened to him.

In times preceding the ones this story is concerned with, there had been great turmoil and upheaval in the country where the Christian girl lived. The man who had been its President Supreme, in other words its head of state, cried tears all day and all night because in his third consecutive campaign to be appointed leader, his opponents and friends had acted craftily and even bought votes, resulting in his painful loss of power. So his side and the other side armed themselves to the teeth and set about causing untold misery and disaster. When divine intervention, or the fact that both sides had run out of money and ammunition, brought the conflict to a standstill, the two factions made friends again and departed the provinces, leaving hundreds of dead bodies in their wake. Once the better placed of the two camps took a firm grip on power, the two sides' wild militias were disbanded. Behind them, a trail of orgies was consigned to painful history. Orgies of blood and orgies of violation, the military uniform the agent between damaged girls and feral boys, children wrenched from sylvan innocence.

From such circumstances did Omar Salanga emerge. It was claimed that he was one of the young guns used by the aspirants to power and that he'd been part of an infantry that rampaged through villages, slaughtering anyone unfortunate enough to cross its path. Some said he'd been born with madness, others that he'd lost his mind having been ordered to spread terror in the bush. Either way, he couldn't live with the terrible things he'd done and so he tried to block out the past with *banga* smoke and cool his aching heart with fresh river water. But why did he not take his boots off? Did he expose his manliness to the elements in order to cool that down too? It was said that he did, and that's why after floating up and down he submerged himself fully in the river before getting out. Many things were said, until the consensus was that the church choir's expedition had been a fiasco from start to finish. First and foremost, the parish priest had assumed that a man with a name like Omar was a recalcitrant Muslim who could be cut down with Christian song, when they might have fared better trying to bring him back into the fold. That's right, he may have been called Omar, but behind the ominous name lay a wayward Christian spirit, providence having set him out on the path of the prodigal son. In other words, instead of confronting him, they'd have been better off sprinkling holy water over the man and sanctifying his manhood for the glory of African Christianity.

But no matter, whether because of the choir's intervention or lack thereof, Omar decided to leave the village beside the river and put his past behind him. Desperate to rid himself of the memories that plagued him, he crossed border after border, resolving to renounce nation and flag, if ever he had them, and emigrate to Europe.

But his legend preceded him and so, wherever a significant number of Africans were gathered waiting to reach for the promised land, whether having crossed a desert or not, there would be an Omar Salanga among them, bearing all the man's virtues and vices on his back. Was it really him or an impostor who'd learned of Omar's death and decided to fill his boots and propagate the myth? All we can say for sure is that Omar Salanga had been in many places, and now he was on Gurugu. Furthermore, he was not alone, rather he'd joined forces with a certain Aliko Dangote. The two of them were responsible for the unrest on the mountain. So who was Aliko Dangote?

IV

'Hi Peter. We have an *acoté* pending and the tournament's been suspended, so maybe now would be a good time to discuss what you said: "until we show them any different, what's written in books will be what's read out on the radio, day and night". Wouldn't you say that's a very sweeping statement to make?'

'Would you say it was sweeping, brother?'

'I'd say your statement draws a line between us and them. We're ignorant, they're clever, is that the way you see it?'

'That depends. Who do you mean by "they"?' asked Peter.

'The whites, no? You seemed to have very clear ideas, so clear you knew what would be read out on the radio each day.'

'Yes, I remember, and yes, I was referring to the whites. Before we carry on, can I ask you where you are from, brother?'

'You can ask, friend, but you probably half know the answer.'

'And what about the other half?'

'You probably know that half too, because this close to the finishing line, we're none of us from anywhere. You know that, right?'

'Yes, I know that, brother, but I also know that no matter where we end up, our heart will forever contain a small piece of our homeland. I would say you are from the Zambezi basin, am I right?'

'I don't know what makes you say that, maybe you're confusing me with someone else who spoke of that place. But OK, let's say I am. Whatever difference that makes.'

'You said I draw a line between us and them. But there will never be whites here, brother, not on this mountain,' said Peter.

'And do you think that's due to them being more intelligent?'

'No.'

'Then do you think it's because they killed more?'

'Saying they killed more only confuses the issue, brother. I do not think killing people has much to do with intelligence.'

'Then what's your basis for saying we must try harder, I don't remember your exact words, but try harder to change what whites say about us on the radio?'

'Can it really be said that whites have killed more?' Peter asked. 'Does the reality of what we are trying to understand here really come down to such a dramatic equation?'

'There are fundamental truths we don't know, and if we knew them, we wouldn't be where we are today.

But the fact of the matter is that whites have killed and killed a lot.'

'As have blacks,' said Peter. 'But if we are to talk about killing, and please do not take offence, brother, I would say whites know why they kill, but blacks often do not.'

'I'm not sure I accept that,' said the man who'd agreed to be from the Zambezi region. 'Try and convince me.'

'I cannot convince you, brother, I can merely present you with the facts that here we are, some five hundred men and women, waiting to break into what we might call a house, and we do not know if we will be welcome in that house. And the house belongs to the whites.'

'Nothing convincing causes offence, so you haven't offended me, friend. But you have missed a key point.'

'And what point might that be?' asked Peter, playing the student.

'Africans, or rather blacks, maybe don't wish to benefit from death.'

'Well, they should do. I am sorry to be crude, but that is the truth of it, for it shows superior wisdom.'

'What you call wisdom might just as easily be called opportunism. I say this because a black man acknowledging white superiority is no small thing.'

'And it is no small thing that hundreds of black men are gathered here, brother, as are thousands of others elsewhere, trying to break into the white man's house.'

'I wouldn't put it in those terms,' said the man from Zambezi.

'Well, how would you put it then? Enlighten me.'

'It should really be you enlightening me, but fine, I'll take up the mantle. I mentioned opportunism, and in doing so I think I hit the nail on the head, but I'll also say this: the black man is pleased with himself.'

'Pleased with himself? You mean the way that I, Peter, am pleased to be black?'

'Something like that,' said the Zambezi man. 'Being happy with your lot means watching things happen without understanding how they impact on your life. That's how we blacks are. We have our jungle, our elephants, our lions, our sitatungas, our snakes, we have thousands of species of vegetable and two enormous rivers, or three, according to my schoolbooks, but we're fresh out of cows, horses and grass, and nobody mentions this, that's what rankles with me. We go on like this, until we experience poverty and then we abandon our villages, we find ourselves here, and if the gods smile kindly upon us, we get over to the other side. Then much later we realise life wasn't so bad with the jungle, the elephants and the rhinos, but this we only learn there, once we're very far away and it's practically impossible to go back.'

'It is a devastating portrait, brother, and I would struggle to come up with a more graphic way of describing the situation.'

'One other thing. Have you heard of African pride?'

'Yes,' replied Peter, eagerly.

'Well, there's no such thing.'

'What?' said Peter with some surprise. 'Are you saying we Africans have nothing to be proud of?'

'No, we have plenty to be proud of,' said the man from the Zambezi. 'But can you imagine a native of the Sahara desert standing in Red Square, Moscow, and talking about African pride?'

'Is this a trick question, brother, or just a particularly strange example?'

'Strange example? Okay then, can you imagine a native of the Zambezi basin talking about African pride in Red Square?'

'Are you saying neither man has anything to be proud of? I know you are trying to highlight a paradox, I am just not sure which one.'

'You're catching on,' said the man from Zambezi with some satisfaction. 'What gets called African pride is nothing but a paradox, because we Africans often no longer have poisonous snakes or giraffes or sitatungas, we have no jungle or access to a river . . . and when I say river, I really mean running water, that there's no running water in people's houses or neighbourhoods. So whenever an African opens his mouth and speaks of African pride and progress, he's left with a bitter taste at the back of his throat, because there's no pride in having lost everything.'

'I am going to need some time to reflect on what you have just said, brother. I mean, to say there is no such thing as African pride, well, that is a bold and sweeping statement too, would you not say?'

'Maybe,' said the man from Zambezi. 'But you tell me what a black man talking to a Russian in Red Square has to be proud of, when he knows there are no great animals left to admire in his homeland?'

'But what has the Russian got to be proud of?'

'Red Square.'

'After all you have said, brother, I am not sure that it comforts me to know you are black and camped out here with a certain plan in mind. It is unlikely anything could persuade our companions to turn back now, but you and your arguments just might.'

'But turn back why?'

'So that they learn to appreciate poisonous snakes, wild boar, rhinoceros and virgin jungle.'

'But maybe I'm the one who needs persuading.'

'Persuading of what, brother?' asked Peter, intrigued.

'That instead of African pride, which is nothing, we learn to be proud of our African character.'

'What is African character?'

'I don't know,' said the man from the Zambezi. 'But while we've been talking, I've realised that we Africans, black Africans, do have something to be proud of.'

'Well, please share this revelation with me, brother, for I am very much in need of it.'

'Africans tend to be proud of being African, and it doesn't matter where they are, Red Square or somewhere even better. They talk of African pride, even though snakes, sitatunga, lions and rhinos no longer exist, because they're still present inside them. Africans are born and see the world in all its glorious splendour, they revel in it and drink it in, but they take it for granted, they walk around with their eyes closed, and when they open them again, it's all gone, but they don't notice, because that first impression became ingrained in them, so ingrained they can summon it up whenever they like and speak of it with pride in faraway places like Red Square.'

'Goddamn it, brother! That is exactly what happens, of course it is!' exclaimed Peter. 'When they closed their eyes to take in the wonder of it all, perhaps while chewing on a piece of cobra, the whites came along and snatched everything away.'

'We don't eat snakes in my family.'

'It is not expressly forbidden in mine, but maybe I was getting carried away.'

'Well, friend, what can I say? This is some *acoté* we've had. But I have to get going, find out what's going on with my team.'

'Okay, but just let me ask you something: Do you think we have spoken like true Africans?'

'I don't know. How are true Africans supposed to speak?' the man from Zambezi asked, puzzled.

'Are we Africans not supposed to be practical people? Is there not something we should do as a consequence of our long discussion?'

'How about I reply with an African proverb?'

'Is concealing our wisdom not part of the problem?' said Peter. 'Would it not be hypocritical?'

'No, friend, I don't think so,' said the man from the Zambezi. 'The proverb, whose authorship has long since been forgotten, although it can be traced way back to the first inhabitants of the Zambezi basin, goes like this: If you get lost in the forest and don't hear friendly voices calling you home, perhaps you shouldn't have left your house in the first place.'

'And what does it mean?'

'It's an old African proverb: if I explained it, we'd be here a very long time.'

'Okay, brother, but maybe we can have another *acoté* another day?' said Peter, trying to read the other man's expression.

'Yes, friend, let's do that,' said the man from the Zambezi.

V

So as not to fear the worst on Gurugu, you had to be as positive as the young Malian who'd traded verbal blows with his Gambian counterpart. He'd spoken of having a profession and he'd finished by saying that what went on in Gambia was better described in Latin. He was alluding to a song sung the world over, and indeed the young Malian sang it to his Gambian colleague, playfully and ironically, of course:

Gaudeamus igitur,
iuvenes dum sumus.
Post iucundam iuventutem,
post molestam senectutem,
nos habebit humus.

Following the Marshall Plan, and after huge efforts had been made to forget about all the bombs dropped on bad guys in two successive wars, great wars no less, Europe began to recover, Great Britain included. As the recovery gathered pace, Europeans acquired special powers to put a price on agricultural products they couldn't grow themselves, and never would be able to grow, even if they turned entire countries into giant greenhouses. In this fashion, they lowered the price of the humble peanut, and with it all its by-products, and in this fashion the poor Gambians got poorer, because, through accident and design, the peanut was their most important product, the thing they most sold abroad. So, in order to survive, the Gambians resorted to tourism. Come and visit me, although I've no peanuts for you to spread on your bread, and no bread either in fact, for wheat won't grow in our humid climate. Englishwomen emerged from the Marshall Plan empowered, but many a young Englishman had perished on the battlefield and those who hadn't were busy dealing with the repercussions of having survived. Life was very different for an eighteen-year-old lad in Banjul. If the experience of dropping bombs on Dresden had left young Englishmen weary, then all the better for the young men of Banjul, for whom tourism was manna, a desert miracle that might now develop into something tastier besides. So let's sing the verse again, *Gaudeamus igitur/ iuvenes dum sumus/ Post iucundam iuventutem/ post molestam senectutem,/ nos habebit humus*. But of course! Why stay in London shivering in the cold and suffering from crises of the domestic, intimate and hormonal kind, when the peanut price has plummeted and you could be enjoying tourist packages over there, packages considered too extreme in some countries? Indulge in a bit of tourism while you still can, before time catches up with you once and for all.

'Young man, do you take Dalila to be your wife, in sickness and in wealth? I'll skip the death do us part bit, for it's self-evident.'

'I do.'

'And you, Dalila, do you take Okumuru Osong for a husband, to have and to hold, in good times and in bed?'

'I certainly do.'

'Then in the name of the Lord Almighty, I pronounce you man and wife. You may now kiss the bride,' announced the priest. 'I said, you may now kiss the bride.'

'Kiss! Kiss! Kiss! Kiss!' chanted the assembled well-wishers.

'Hey, why are they taking so long to kiss?' said someone who'd been passing by and called in as a witness, witness to a spectacle that was astonishing, but now commonplace in Banjul.

'You have to be motivated, I guess, sufficiently motivated,' the other witness replied. 'Because the bride . . . '

'What about the bride?' said the first witness.

'Kiss! Kiss! Kiss! Kiss! Kiss! Kiss! Kiss! Kiss! Kiss! Kiss! Kiss-kiss-kiss-kiss-kiss! K. I. S. S! K. I. S. S! Kissssssssssssssssssss! Kissssssssssssssssssssssssss! Kissssssssssssssssssssssssss!'

'What about the bride? Oh, nothing, the price of peanuts fell, that's all. When the peanut price falls, the first kiss takes a little while coming.'

VI

The man accused of being Omar's accomplice was Aliko Dangote, or at least that's the name he went by. He hadn't acquired mythical status like his associate, and his backstory wasn't nearly as colourful, maybe because he grew up somewhere without a river and a parish priest in charge of a choir. But he still had a history, of course, and what he was accused of ensured that his past went under the magnifying glass. Indeed Gurugu nearly burned because of it.

That's when the decision was taken to suspend the football tournament, something that would not have happened for no good reason, given the times they were living through. The same good reason was why two Gurugu residents had to ask for something their sisters needed when they went into the villages to beg for food. They were told they'd have to try a shop, because in the houses they called at nobody used the item scribbled down on a piece of paper. Besides, why would a woman, be she a Moroccan local or a visiting Bedouin, a Spanish *señorita* escaped from Cádiz or a French *mademoiselle* enchanted by the Barbary coast, wish to share personal information about being on her period or having reached the menopause or had a hysterectomy or whatever, with two black male strangers? The two men went back up the hill empty-handed, or without the item in question at least, for they had two potatoes and a handful of onions, a few of which they had to give to the men who welcomed newcomers to the camp and made decisions.

After the first match had been suspended, the tension grew and rumours took root in different corners of the camp. The mood was so fraught that a lot of people forgot about the circumstances they lived in, the precarious nature of their existence and the severity with which the Kingdom of Morocco's police were prone to act. If tempers flared in the camp, the police would have the perfect excuse for a crackdown and their actions would go totally uncontested. No dissenting voices would come from the north or south, there would be silence from the west and if the east managed a murmur of protest, it would soon be drowned out by bigger news, a mass shipment of cocaine seized in a nearby port perhaps.

The four-nations tournament didn't take place because before the sun had come up on the Algerian horizon, an incident had occurred in one of the caves at the top, a cave known as the residence. It was occupied by a mixture of old hands and new arrivals from greener parts of Africa. Yes, green. In that cave there were many men and a few women. All the floor space was occupied, but an uneasy harmony held, at least until the first match was suspended and home truths had to be confronted. A veil had been drawn over something from the start, and there was a will to likewise shield its ending. In other words, the residents wished to deal with the consequences in the dark, out of sight from indiscreet eyes.

As night drew in and teeth began to chatter, four men made their way down the mountain carrying two women on their backs. They came from the residence, but took a loop and went the long way round. They weren't trying to hide what they were doing, but they didn't want to invite unnecessary questions: the fewer questions they had to answer, the quicker they would reach their destination. Two women carried on the backs of two men, with two other men ready to take turns. They were going in search of help, help for the women, who were unwell.

The women became unwell after the cave had become so crowded that no one else would fit in it, there was no more floor space. The next arrivals would have to look elsewhere, or build tents out of whatever they could find. 'I'm going to lie down here next to you, Shania, no disrespect to you and your husband, I don't mean to be so close, but there's no alternative, the tent distribution scheme hasn't reached us yet, so don't mind me.' A moment's silence, then 'Fine, just don't mind what you see, brother.' That was the deal, man-to-man, a deal in which the husband was complicit, although at the time some people thought he was the brother, Shania's older brother, and so he got to decide things for her, as that was the way things were and were meant to be. And so a veil was drawn over certain activities. The residents began to detect odours that surface when adult men cross a large desert and end up on an isolated mountain. But there was a veil.

A veil. Sniff, I smell someone's insides, or something rotten. There are a lot of men in here, of course, and there are even two women, but don't women have a better sense of smell than men? Why don't the women complain? Yes, why don't they complain if I'm about to? Something stinks around here, something hidden, I don't know what it is, but it gets worse at night. I'm going to have to go to the mouth of the cave to get some air. It smells there too, but not so bad you can't sleep.

'What is that awful smell?'

'Ah, I don't know, what do you think it is?'

Well, there are no wash facilities for women and we've got two who've travelled through a desert to get here. What little water we have is for drinking, and it's cold. If there were a big bucket, maybe we could fill it with water, warm it on the fire and the women could take turns showering. But there is no big bucket, so our noses bristle and detect a certain scent.

'Overcrowding, brother.'

'And what else?'

'Despair.'

'And what else?'

Well, nobody will say it, but the smell is particularly strong near sister Shania, the nearest person to me in the cave.

'The lack of water. If there were a river where everyone could – '

'Ah, if there were a river of warm water we'd be the happiest blacks in Africa. But there isn't. Shall we raise the matter with our brothers?'

'I'd rather not, I don't wish to speak ill of our sisters.'

'I don't wish to speak ill of anybody.'

For the inhabitants of Gurugu, the lack of everything was a constant, but that one of the women was suffering badly from a lack of water became impossible to ignore.

'So, what are we going to do? It's too cold to abandon the cave and sleep outside.'

'Let's say something to her brother in private.'

'Somebody already has.'

'Really?'

'Really.'

Such was the state of affairs the day the match was suspended. Everyone, in their own particular way, sought reasons for the suspension. Very few people knew of the expedition down the hill, two women carried on two men's backs. The women were very sick. They'd been sick for several days, had got gradually worse and were finally carried down the hill in the dark. When they got to the lower reaches of the mountain, they made their presence felt: they wanted the authorities, any authorities, anyone with power, including the Moroccan forestry police, to hear them, to ask them what they were doing and listen to their story, to pity them and take the two women to hospital, where their ills would have been diagnosed and they would have received help. But the men either took the wrong path or simply weren't seen or heard by the authorities, any authorities. They got all the way down the hill and as far as the main gate to the brightest of the nearby towns, but as they approached the gate there was a bend in the track and they were suddenly blinded by the powerful light of a torch.

'What are you doing down here? Why's your back covered in blood? What filthy shit have you been up to now?'

'No, brother, please, we have been carrying two sick women, we are taking them to the – '

'Taking them where? What makes you think there's a hospital for blacks anywhere in this country?'

'Our sisters are very sick, we've no medicine for them.'

'We've no medicine for them either. And anyway, you can't walk along these paths at night, you know the rules.'

'We do, but they are seriously sick, please, for the love of God.'

'Liars! Get back! Where are these sick women anyway?'

'Right behind us, carried by two of our brothers. Please!'

'Please? Kidnap and human trafficking are serious crimes.'

The forestry police proved to be in a particularly vindictive mood that night. Their wickedness was given free rein as they got out their truncheons and showed off their guns, and then used them. Used them with pleasure and impunity. They did whatever they wanted, whatever popped into their twisted heads, and it was ugly. Two of the men managed to escape, leaving the other two, along with the two women, alone in enemy territory. The women never made it to a health centre, ambulance, shelter or mosque. Anywhere someone might have taken them in was too far away, beyond their grasp and energies. When news of the devastating outcome of this failed mission reached camp the next day, it was the spark that lit the fuse that nearly set the mountain ablaze. Outrage brought two names to everyone's lips: Omar Salanga and Aliko Dangote.

Those familiar with the camp knew that some people were sent to the upper part, some to the middle part, some to the lower part, but they also knew that others went everywhere and decided where everyone else was supposed to go. Such people knew all the team captains and they talked to them. They were people who had been in many countries and spoke at least two languages. Or only spoke one, but acted like they spoke others. And when these people saw Gurugu inhabitants who were in some way pained, it was as if they had emissaries who'd already informed them of the pain and its causes. Everyone on the mountain had come from faraway places seeking a particular path. But no matter how far they'd walked, no matter how much they'd suffered, no matter how much nature had forced them to forget themselves, there came a moment when their sense of smell sharpened and their nose began to detect something. They smelled more than they should have done and they thought it was because many months had passed since they'd last been so close to a woman. If the thoughts that followed had been articulated, many curious tales would have come out, tales the tellers would have disowned if they'd ever found their way back to the villages they'd come from. In a cave on the top of a mountain they discovered they were men, real men, fully grown men, and that they could smell more than the situation required. But others had realised this before them, which is why things happened – happened and had a veil drawn over them.

Of course, in a cave on top of a mountain it's not easy to put up veils, especially when some are quicker than others to realise that men are men, flesh and blood, and especially when those who realise have eyes and a tendency to look, for then they see more than they'd like to see and they realise that a man's small needs can lead him into big traps. Traps likes the ones encountered on paths through the desert. Those with eyes look and they understand that those who know the desert's paths and traps can take advantage of that knowledge, which is what Aliko Dangote did. That wasn't his real name. The man that name actually belonged to was a successful businessman in Nigeria who'd started out selling cardboard boxes on the street, worked hard, applied himself, found backers and become the richest man in Nigeria before he'd even chalked up half a century. Aliko the Rich, they called him. The best part of half a century buying and selling all over Africa and there he was, on the Forbes list of millionaires, among the filthy rich. Private cars, mansions, aeroplanes; bank accounts with lots of zeros: 0000000 . . . His name became so well known that even in the desert, pathfinders adopted it hoping that some of his magic might rub off on them, even just a little bit. That's how our Aliko Dangote came into being, a young man eager to make his fortune, as well equipped as the original Aliko, just not as lucky. But he found his calling as a pathfinder and he took every advantage the role presented, and soon Christians were crossing themselves out of fear whenever they encountered him.

You got to the Gurugu camp and you were received by someone who knew your language, someone who encouraged you to keep your spirits up and remember your survival instincts. Later on, that same someone would tell you what you had to do. So it became clear that those who'd arrived first got to decide things and, if you were a woman, make decisions for you, because women were such delicate little things, especially on desert paths, all kinds of paths through all kinds of deserts. You're a woman, you've just arrived, you settle in and you start to see things, and you go on seeing them and you realise you're a woman and that men find it hard to live like eunuchs.

Before the source of the stink became known, or the need to know became imperative, those on the mountain who went about with their eyes open saw that certain people had power over others. Even more so than they'd originally thought. They noticed that Aliko would come along and make a gesture and that someone would respond, as if he were able to exercise his power at the flick of a switch, and as if this was normal. It became a cause of confusion. Wasn't that man Shania had come with supposed to be her husband? And if not her husband, her brother, or someone she shared intimate words with at least? Her companions in the cave started to notice things. Or sense them, smell them. Because you've travelled all the way from your country just like everyone else, you've worked en route, catching fish or unloading Chinese lorries in foreign lands, and you've dug deep into your pockets and worked and saved whatever it cost to keep going, until you reached the least racist point for miles around, the camp on Mount Gurugu. One night you find yourself lying a few feet away from a woman who covers her head to go to sleep, because the nights are cool, and you see someone enter the cave, someone lit up by the light of . . . a mobile phone! The person comes over to where the woman is sleeping, taps her gently on the shoulder, lest she take fright and wake up the whole cave, and then the two of them leave the cave and something flickers in your head, or two things do. Yes, two things, because first you ask yourself when you last felt like a man and secondly you wonder whether the man who's officially her husband has seen what you've just seen, even whether you perhaps ought to cough so that he stirs and realises that someone in the camp has a fully charged mobile phone. How many people on the mountain had an operational phone, ready to receive calls? Very few, if any at all, because the nearest city with electricity was not a friendly place, so unless you found a bus station or a bar somewhere that was prepared to let you plug into its supply, your phone's battery would be flat.

The flicker in your head grows, because you see another brother making his way towards Shania in the dark, and you think you're the only one who sees it, this time you even cough so that there might be other witnesses or so that the husband might wake, but the intruder gets what he wants, he knows what he's come for. And then a light goes on in your head and you feel as though you're the one who's being cheated, even though you're not the husband or even a distant cousin of his, he who sleeps so deeply. And you curse your lot, and you even start to wonder whether it would be too much to ask for her to attend to her own group first, before some intruder with a fully charged mobile phone has a go. And you feel utterly despondent the next morning when no one mentions it, as if it never happened. Those whose turn it is to get water set off, those whose turn it is to gather firewood get down to it, and those whose turn it is to go begging head for the villages. All as if nothing happened!

First you get a sinking feeling, then pity kicks in and you wonder what lurks behind this nocturnal business. This noxious business. The days pass and you realise that what you'd thought was a one-off happens every night, but still you don't know what to say. Is he her husband or not? You have many questions, and you wonder if there are some things men can't stop themselves from doing.

Hours pass and the tension mounts and most people don't know what's going on, who's sick, why are they sick, what's troubling everyone, why has the tournament been suspended. And you start speculating and you wonder how many people on the mountain have a fully functioning mobile phone, given that there's no electricity for miles around, and the nearest city with electricity doesn't count, because you cannot enter it. The hours pass and the truth starts to come out. A name emerges: Aliko; that rich guy. So rich, in fact, that he'd be one of very few people likely to have a mobile phone. Someone else might have one, but never get it out, for opportunities to connect to an electricity source were few and the chances of getting hold of a phone card for the country that owned the mountain were practically non-existent. So who was Aliko? Just an unaccompanied man who'd been appointed a team captain. A man who exemplified what it meant to be rich nowadays: when nobody has anything, someone has everything. So who was the man behind the celebrated name? He didn't say much, or if he did he spoke only to those of equal standing. He was bilingual, and he had power and influence and enough resources to charge a mobile phone when there was no electricity on the mountain, meaning he regularly went into the nearby villages, or had someone go for him, and he had the means to get what he wanted down there.

Tempers were fraying and the mountain was on the verge of being set on fire. The camp veterans decided to meet. They did so discreetly, choosing the most inaccessible part of the mountain. The man who took charge adopted a very African attitude to dealing with serious problems: he sought the most rugged crag, somewhere it would be easy to lose your footing, and he summoned the two men who'd been singled out by the other inhabitants, or by a significant number of them at least. Two men whose lives were understood to be in danger. By summoning them to somewhere you could easily lose your footing, the implication was that if they were found guilty, they'd have to fight for their lives, they weren't going to be handed over to the Moroccan forestry police. Everything would be resolved there and then, in a place where it was very easy to slip. The whole community would soon learn who the fake Aliko really was and what role he'd played in that unseemly saga, a saga in which he'd had a dangerous man for an accomplice and for which they'd be judged together.

Why was a married woman woken in the middle of the night and led out into the forest to attend to some unsavoury business? That was the first question that needed answering. Only then could the husband regain his honour, or be condemned with the other two. Next came the question of what the woman had done to warrant such treatment, a young woman who'd left her village and home to join the adventure.

Well, the fake Aliko was nobody, he had no illustrious past or origins, he just worked hard to get people's attention. One of his schemes came good, or rather he struck a lucky blow on a desert crossing, earning him a sort of respect. He rescued a number of people from danger. Or maybe he put their lives at risk, he never let it be known and so we must rely on what others have said. He took part in long walks in search of lost dignity, setting off without a compass or a map, but with the conviction that doors would open on the other side, whatever doors they might be, and if they didn't open, that they could be broken down. Only the strongest survive such journeys, the better equipped, those with the most resources. Those like Aliko, who had the advantage of travelling alone, unlike Shania's husband, who hadn't been able to persuade his wife to stay at home and wait for him to return. They'd sacrificed their past for a future, and a present in a cave with night-time visits the husband felt obliged to ignore. What kind of pact had he made whereby men could drag his wife out of bed in the night and expose her to the cold mountain air? Were such murky goings-on merely the price you paid for giving it all up, for leaving nothing behind? Otherwise, he would have surely turned back and made for home the first time a man came along and told him to look the other way. Made for home hurting and with his head bowed.

Shania's story went like this: a group of several men and a few women travelled north until they came to a door that was very hard to get through. The door was one of hundreds of frontier checkpoints set up by bandits along African paths, bandits dressed in official uniform, but accountable to nobody. Sorry, but you're not going through, said the supervisor. Then: Where are your papers? He asked just for the fun of it, just to hassle, to intimidate, to frighten. Documents were duly produced, and then the supervisor noticed there was a woman among the travelling men, and he suddenly became exercised and upset.

He was upset by one of the papers, a document that he himself, or one of his colleagues, had forged previously, for that's how they earned their corn. So he took Shania into a squalid room full of nauseating smells and he shut the door behind her. Stains on the wall and scars on the door spoke of past horrors endured by earlier prisoners, while horrifying insects wallowed in the filth and stench. The rest of the group didn't know what to do. But then one of them, as if the whole business of leaving the country barely concerned him, approached the bandits and addressed them in their own language. He was a young man and he knew many vernaculars. Come on, guys, don't fuck me around, you planning on having the girl for tea or what? Speak in as many tongues as you like, we've got a job to do and this isn't the first time you've tried to pull a fast one on us. Say now, I didn't want to call it a bribe, so as not to upset you, but how much is it going to cost to resolve this little problem? Ask the boss. Who's that? Him over there. Really, because I thought the minister had final say on these things, so why don't we give him a call? The minister's busy with more important matters, so don't try to be clever. I see. Yes, he must be very busy.

Shania's husband didn't know what to do and they could all see the guards sharpening their tools ready for the feast that would commence as soon as there was a lull in the traffic and trafficking. So the young man got serious and he went over to the boss and he took him to one side, as if he wanted to talk to him about genealogy and the history of black people, from General Hanno to

Shaka Zulu. They talked for a while, the husband didn't know what to do, the young man returned to the group, and still nothing happened, and then the young man took the boss into his cabin of an office. He didn't want to waste any more time, but he didn't want to call the man's bluff and risk upsetting him either. They came out of the office and the boss opened the door to the putrid cell. There they found Shania, tears streaming down her cheeks, her whole being enveloped in a thousand disgusting smells. She'd soiled herself. That's right, she'd been so afraid of being left alone with those people, for they had a very bad reputation, that she'd defecated in her pants. She'd have been imprisoned there and only let out when they caught another woman, someone fresher and in better condition. But the door had opened and now she was free. She said not a word to anyone about having sullied her pants and they set off walking. She let the others get a little way ahead, or she said she was hanging back to relieve herself, and then she took off her trousers and removed the knickers that contained the product of her terror. She put her trousers back on and left the knickers by the path. The next expedition of black men heading north would find them and someone would wonder what had happened for someone to have left them there. What could have happened for a woman to lose, so far away from any town or village, her most intimate garment?

They went on walking, Shania and her husband and the rest of their companions, and at some point chance brought the young man alongside her, the young man who'd negotiated her freedom. He consoled her and he said not to worry, that in the first village they came to he'd find a shop and buy her a new pair of knickers. He wouldn't forget, he said, it was a promise.

They walked and walked until they were beyond exhaustion, and they covered many miles and many things happened, things none of them can remember, but which remain buried at the bottom of their hearts. Through much sweat and suffering, they reached the mountain, whereupon they were sent to a cave known as the residence. Shania's saviour joined others elsewhere in the camp, his speaking several languages deemed to be an important advantage. But he hadn't forgotten the promise he'd made during the crossing. There was no shop on the mountain, so he kept hold of the promise, and then he started taking advantage of it. This was allowed to happen because the black men who'd renounced their African lives were not made of stone; they were beings, with beating hearts, and needs. They were men. They'd been through so much and they knew more was to come. They sensed something, something important and painful, something they couldn't fight, for they sensed that the further north they got, the lesser were their chances of feeling like a man again. They would be forever on their feet, part of a collective mass. This they sensed, or concluded from the stories they'd heard.

There was no shop on the mountain and the only form of commerce was a barter economy, I'll give you this for that, deals done amongst friends, a trade in survival items. And so the promise became a threat. Her husband felt weak, he had no resources, he was indebted to his wife's saviour and couldn't counter his threat, so he succumbed to the other man's will in the hope that normality would thus be restored. Nobody could testify to the deal, but some saw it acted upon. In the first village we come to, I'll buy you new knickers. What kind of person buys knickers for a woman he's not related to? And so he started calling in the debt instead. Go up there, ask for Shania's cave, tell her I sent you.

'Why are you doing this, brother?'

'Bah, she owes me, I did her a big favour. If it weren't for me . . . '

'But get her husband to pay you back.'

'Say now, if it weren't for me, she'd have been left to a bunch of racist, rapist soldiers. They'd have had their way with her for hours on end, until they were sapped of all energy, and then they'd have tossed her out like a used rag. Do you know how many infected women pass through here?'

Tell her I sent you. No, it's not a problem. Just make sure it's her and not the other one. Yeah. Tell her I sent you, it'll be no problem. Yeah. Tell her, tell her I sent you. Yeah, thanks. Just tell her I sent you, Aliko, yeah, got it?

'How much?'

'Don't fuck me around.'

'I'm not, I just don't know how much it is, alright.'

'Bah, how much have you got?'

Okay, give it here. Tell her I sent you. You use the light of the phone, you step between the bodies sprawled on the ground, lying on cardboard boxes, covered in MSF blankets, and you find her and you make her get up from where she's got warm and you take her out into the cold and you do the deed.

Remember, I'll buy you a new pair of knickers in the first village we come to, only then will you be able to forget the ones you threw away loaded with your own shit. That's how Aliko called in the debt, how he made the girl pay him back for rescuing her from the checkpoint guards as they crossed the desert. And when the Gurugu inhabitants risked everything to get to the truth and punish those who were to blame, people said the husband who never spoke up and played dumb was guilty too. How could he not have tried to do something to pay his wife, lover, girlfriend or bride-to-be's debt? They asked whether he was even really her husband and not perhaps a brother exploiting his own sister, or else a boyfriend collaborating with others, soliciting his girlfriend's services? They said this because they couldn't believe that any man born in the Africa they knew could be so spiritless and spineless. Yes, spiritless and spineless were the words they used.

'The way I see it, if that man's wife, poor sister, had incurred a debt, then he should have paid it.'

'But how, eh?'

'Ah, he could have promised to pay him back, or paid him back by working for him. Or just given him some kind of assurance the debt would be paid.'

'Do you know something I don't know, brother? Because I can't see how a man can pay another man back when he hasn't any money or anything to barter with.'

'You didn't understand what I said, eh?'

'Explain what you meant and I'll tell you if I understood.'

'You want me to spell it out, eh? Look, there are around five hundred people in this forest, only around twenty of whom are women. Want to do the maths of how many to each one? Do the sums, then add on everyone we haven't counted, because this is a big mountain, and then think about it . . . '

'And?'

'Draw your own conclusions. I haven't even mentioned that some women might already be attached or sick.'

'I don't know what you mean by this. We haven't come here to marry the womenfolk! I think maybe your head is full of white people's ideas, because our ancestral African culture is very clear about what's normal.'

'I'm not sure what African culture even is, dear brother.'

'Fine, just don't get any funny ideas, and especially not with me. Just because we're somewhere where there aren't many women doesn't mean anything goes. We haven't even reached Europe yet and your head's already corrupted.'

'Well, I'm sorry if I offended you. Just don't be surprised by what you might see.'

That conversation was like a warning shot, for the two men discussing African culture and what was normal very nearly came to blows. No doubt they would have done if it hadn't been for an even more explosive discussion developing further down the hill. A group of young men were arguing vociferously about the best way to deal with a situation that now had names and surnames attached to it. Some thought that what Aliko Dangote and Omar Salanga had done deserved the utmost punishment. Besides, the one who called himself Aliko was masquerading as someone else, a man who'd got where he had through hard work. They also spoke of the women, the two women who'd been carried down the hill in search of help.

VII

The sick women didn't make it to anywhere that could have helped them, not even an MSF first-aid unit that might have enquired as to what was wrong. The mobile first-aid unit wasn't anywhere to be seen and the expedition was cut short by a group of Moroccan police officers. Two men fled and the other two were left for dead with the women. It was the middle of the night and the forest was pitch black, although there were lights aplenty in the town ahead. With tremendous difficulty, the two men who'd been left behind managed to carry the women back into the forest and a little way up the hill. When they reached a dry gorge where a stream had once flowed, they lowered the women to the ground and collapsed. The women couldn't walk, the men barely could, and they were in a remote part of the forest, a place not usually frequented by those in the Gurugu camp; it was unlikely anyone would come to their aid. Stunned by the turn of events and the truncheon blows, the men had likely become disorientated and lost their way. They had come to rest in a place they'd never been to before, and there they would stay, panting and whimpering, the two women in terrible pain, the two men with their battered bodies.

The next morning, they heard war cries coming from further up the mountain. The argument the young men were having in the middle part of the camp had become so animated that its echoes reached them, a rumble brought in on the wind beneath the rustle of the leaves. The two women and the two men knew something serious was happening, and they later learned it was an attempt to teach Omar Salanga an everlasting lesson. They didn't know that then, but they were nevertheless alarmed, because whatever it was could be heard at the bottom of the hill and that jeopardised the lives of everyone. The fate of the entire camp ultimately lay in the hands of the Moroccan forestry police, for they were the nearest legal authority, and if some outrage occurred, even to the camp's most notorious inhabitant, the police would see it as an invitation to invade. A group within the Gurugu camp was trying to right a serious wrong, but its actions risked making the situation far worse, because the police would have liked nothing better than to raze the camp and clear the mountain of black people, and if the black people themselves gave them the excuse to do so, all the better. The camp's very existence therefore hung in the balance as the young men argued over the lesser of two evils: they either spared Omar the punishment he so richly deserved or they punished him and suffered the consequences, consequences that came in the form of the Moroccan forestry police. On the rugged crag, those who knew the finer points of the case ruled that Omar deserved the severest of penalties.

Such was the story of Aliko and the restoration of Shania's knickers: Madame or Miss, I'll address you as I please, and yes, I promised to buy you a new pair of knickers, for you could hardly go on wearing your old ones, full of shit as they were. Full of your own filth, because what would you have said at the next checkpoint when the guards asked you about the smell emanating from your tatty old handbag? You wouldn't have been let in anywhere stinking like that, except maybe your own home. I'll keep my promise, but until then your husband answers to me, because I spared him the pain of having to answer for what would have happened to you. He owes me. So I'm asking you to attend to Raymundi, Konaré, Cissé, Max Kemba, Djibril, Daniel Umó . . . as well as all the others you attend of your own account, for I know what you women are like, you can't help yourselves. I don't care whether your husband knows, it's not my fault life's hard. I'm just calling in my debt, I mean no harm to anybody. I'm just trying to get you your knickers back.

And so on. Things continued in this vein until Omar arrived on the mountain. Was it really him or someone who'd adopted his name and backstory? That could easily have been the case, or maybe it was a different person who'd acted in the same way but in a different place, someone who even looked like him and shared certain physical attributes. Whoever he was, he arrived on the mountain and learned who was running the show, who had something to sell. You might be following your dreams, but you don't stop feeling like a man, and maybe that feeling must come to the surface now and again, because you don't know what your life will be when you reach your destination, or even if you'll reach it. Hey, Aliko, I want use of the woman you keep. I keep only a promise, brother. Fine, give me the promise then. It's all yours, for a fixed price, tell her I sent you.

It was the story of how some Africans grab other Africans by the throat and rub their faces in the misery they've created for themselves, while others watch on or applaud.

Omar, whether in person or in spirit, arrived on the mountain, and he arrived with a thirst. Tell her I sent you. The story of how some grab others by the throat might have ended there, had that man with the thirst not been who he was. Omar, or someone claiming to be him, took Shania away and mistreated her, then did the same with her companion, a woman whose life and secrets we know little about. Shania was too slight a woman in too fragile a state for a volatile and frequently intoxicated man like Omar to abuse without doing fatal damage. Omar, we're going to kill you, you'll die before the women do.

The story of the restitution of Shania's knickers could naturally be told a different way. The way it happened, for example, step by step, blow by blow, seen from the inside: Hello, girl, your creditor sent me, come outside and we'll find a secluded place in the dark and cold bushes and you can pay off your debt. But he's sent so many already, my private parts have started to protest, although I'm too ashamed to speak of what happened. Has gone on happening. I've lost my voice. What about my husband? Well, I said private parts, but the sky was my roof and the trees my witnesses. What about my husband! What will be, will be. All I know is Omar almost made me forget my objective, and my objective remains the same, to go on living, to go on living and answer destiny's call. I can't speak, but I must:

'Do you hear that, sister?'

'I have ears.'

'What will we do?'

'Bah, what will others do for us, sister Shania? We can but hope all the screaming doesn't stop them coming for us, because something serious must be happening if we can hear it down here. If I don't get up again, tell my mother I did nothing wrong, and ask her to take care of my children.'

A great ruckus ripped through the occupied part of the mountain, despite attempts to contain the aggression by those who feared attracting police attention. By the time it was over and tempers had calmed, Shania had discharged the foetus that had been growing inside her. Repeated exposure to vaginal violence presumed, unviable products of conception demonstrable. The blood congealed and stemmed the flow, leaving her clinging to life by a thread, in a dry riverbed at the bottom of Mount Gurugu.

The two men who'd been left for dead made it back to camp and confirmed the story their colleagues had told, the two men who'd escaped amidst the police beating and returned at first light. The two stragglers, bruised and battered, then described the location of the riverbed and a search party struck out to recover the women.

'What happened to Omar and Aliko in the end?'

'They were saved by their religion, brother.'

'They were religious?'

'They said they were.'

'And there we were thinking we'd seen it all, that we could no longer be shocked by the evils of men. What about Shania's husband, eh?'

'He ran away. He was going to be lynched along with Aliko.'

'But he was innocent.'

'That depends on how you look at it, brother. Listen, there was once a boat that came to dock in Mombasa, to fill up its water tanks. It was a normal boat, but its passengers had strange faces and wore striking clothes, although they hardly let themselves be seen. They barely left their cabins, but when they did half-open their doors, smoke rushed out into the light and flooded the air. And if you sneaked a peek through the doors, you saw that the passengers really were curious looking, and you saw that there were lots of women on board, extremely beautiful women who would appear to have deserved better than those men, whose noses were as sharp and crooked as their cutlasses. A trader decided to take advantage of the boat's stay in that great harbour of the African Indian Ocean, and so he approached the ship and asked to see the cook. They talked and he offered the cook a large batch of crabs, saying they were so fine a delicacy that only the most distinguished members of society could appreciate them, people of the calibre of the passengers on that ship. As an aside, and guessing at the true nature of the voyage, for he'd chanced a glimpse through a door, the trader added that invertebrate crustaceans had very powerful aphrodisiac properties, properties the boat's esteemed passengers would surely appreciate. The cook was won over and bought the whole consignment. Everything on that voyage was of the highest quality and the cook wanted his dishes to live up to the high standards set by the passengers. He took the crabs into the kitchen and he rubbed his hands with glee, for he would apply his superior culinary skills to nature's great harvest and rapture the passengers' taste buds. Meanwhile, smoke billowed out of the cabins every time a door opened a crack, a sign of the exuberance and vice within. The cook excelled himself and the gastronomic masterpieces he served were duly gorged upon and praised. A few hours later, the moorings were pulled in and the boat pulled out into the open sea. Darkness fell and when night was at its thickest, the ship's passengers, the beautiful ladies and their mysterious gentlemen companions with their angular features and well-kept beards, were all to be found leaning over the side of the boat making agonising attempts to expel the contents of their stomachs into the ocean. Discreet doses of a potent poison had been inserted into the crustaceans' insides before being handed over to the cook to perform his culinary magic. As the passengers battled against their bellies and the waves, their grip on life and the ship's railings slowly slipping away, a cloaked individual emerged from the shadows, grabbed them by the legs and tipped them overboard, down into the ocean and a fatal encounter with a school of sharks. It's said that the hooded man had boarded the ship in the full knowledge that hundreds of sharks would be passing that day, migrating from the distant shores of Saint Helena to go to spawn at the Andaman Islands. It was, therefore, an ideal opportunity to fulfil a death vow he'd made upon those men, for reasons that remain unclear.'

'Why have you told me this story, brother?'

'Because any one of the passengers on that boat might have been innocent, just like Shania's husband.'

'I'm not sure I understand you. If I'm shaking my head, brother, it's because I really don't see the connection between the two stories. What's the boat got to do with Shania's husband?'

'Well, just as there was one cloaked man intent on murdering everyone in the dark on that pleasure cruise, one gumbooted man determined to ruin things for everyone in that cave. There are many men on this mountain as innocent as Shania's husband, brother, for there are infinite numbers of innocents in the world, each one as innocent as the *Common Birgus latro*.'

By the time night set in, the women had been found and everyone in the camp was aware of the aggravated miscarriage. There was nothing left to say. Nobody had the will to eat or drink or even organise a game of football. Those from the lower parts of the mountain met and made important decisions. There would be a solemn burial for the only human being ever to have been born on the mountain, albeit born with its eyes closed and without ever actually *being*. They gathered cardboard and leaves and made a tiny coffin, big enough for a body that had never properly formed. They put the bloody remains of what Shania's body had expelled inside the makeshift coffin, then carried the coffin out into the middle of the football pitch, the flattest plot of land on Gurugu. They waited until night had fully fallen, so that those who'd come to mourn could do so unobserved, then the five captains said a few words in their respective languages, words of farewell to the little African who'd been born amongst them. They dug a grave and placed the tiny coffin at the bottom. The mother wasn't present, most people didn't know where she was. They pushed the soil back over the coffin and began to fill in the hole. It was now the middle of the night.

Returning to matters of this earth, one of the veterans announced that the suspended football tournament would take place the following day and that everyone should be prepared, everyone. Those levelling the ground where the tomb had been dug performed their work with extra purpose, and others began to join in, the circle enlarging as they sought to make the field of play as flat as possible. It was night, it was terribly cold, teeth chattered, and so more people came to join in, stamping the ground with their feet. Soon, almost everyone was engaged in the task, stamping the ground with their strongest foot, a show of unity after the great pain they'd all suffered.

Because it was night, it was impossible to see people's faces and read their expressions, but they never stopped stamping the ground. They stamped in time, together, so that everyone on the mountain would have heard the pounding, as if someone was beating their chest in a show of remorse or renewed conviction. It was as if nature was responding to a collective trauma, or some communal emotion had taken hold of all of them and compelled them to pummel the earth, and to do so for several minutes, hours even, to the extent that an outsider would have found the whole emotional outpouring strange and unnerving. It was then that they made the pledge. Without stopping the stamping of their feet, and unified by a great sense of solidarity, they closed their eyes and one of the veterans pronounced words that reflected their deep, collective will, and they all responded by pounding the earth even harder, rhythmically and emotionally in synch, and they repeated it until there could be no doubt as to what all this entailed. The veteran's words were brief, intense and passionate; they spoke of the history of Africa and recalled the continent's most significant events. Tears fell from many people's eyes and splashed the earth, but nobody stopped stamping their feet. They stamped and stamped until the night had matured and turned old.

Close to dawn, before the Moroccan police had taken up their positions in front of a fence on a border that had once been open for people to come and go as they pleased, hundreds of Gurugu inhabitants climbed the fence. They were determined to get over and into the city and something about their determination, or some other force not easily understood, meant that those Africans who'd already managed the feat now approached the fence from the other side. Perhaps all those minutes and hours spent stamping the earth had communicated what was happening to them. Whatever it was, the Melilla Africans came to the fence, and they did so just as the Spanish border control police arrived on the scene, kitted out to confront an invading army. As if a certain synergy had been established by the earlier stamping, the Africans on Spanish soil, overflowing with emotion and welling up with tears, began to chant words of encouragement to their companions on the other side. Or a word of encouragement, one word chosen out of all their respective languages, but a word that was understood by everyone, or practically everyone, and that they began to shout in a single voice, their hands raised in a clenched fist: *Bosa! Bosa! Bosa! Bosa! Bosa! Bosa! Bosa! Bosa! Bosa!* One word that meant victory. Victory. That was the message that greeted the zealous Spanish police, and they tried to silence it, but the Africans in Spain wouldn't relent: *Bosa, Bosa, Bosa, Bosa! Bosa! Bosa! Bosa! Bosa! Bosa!! Bosa!! Bosa!! Bosa!!*

On the Gurugu side of the fence, the Moroccan police swung their truncheons, making a great show of it. On the Melilla side, the Spanish police began to get twitchy, as they relayed events via their radios. Up on the fence, clinging and clambering as best they could, dozens of Africans became increasingly elated because they were nearly over and would soon face the final hurdle, albeit a final hurdle made of barbed wire, and so maybe they were about to set foot in Europe, that very African patch of Europe, the nearest bit of Europe to all of them. Nothing could have made them turn back now, nothing could have stopped them, not when they had just a few feet to go. A few difficult feet, to be sure, for they featured a barrier of reinforced barbed wire. *Bosa! Bosa! Bosa! Bosa! Bosa! Bosa! Bosa! Bosa!* chanted the Africans on the Spanish side, in a mixture of euphoria and tears.

The hours passed and the sun rose red over the horizon in the east, kissing houses on the European side, where news of the 'mass storming' of the fence had already spread. The early morning bulletins made a big deal of the matter and included a photo, several photos. Hours passed and anyone looking at the fence in the first light would have noticed two shapes on top of it. They had one leg either side of the fence, as if they were riding a strange horse, a horse with a spiky rump and razor-blades for a mane. The shapes were people, two of the hundreds of Africans who'd taken part in the collective scaling of the fence. But they'd remained there. They made no attempt to advance, nor showed any sign of turning back, their mission having failed. Down below, on the Spanish side, the police waited, all the while explaining what had transpired to the media and their equipment. On the Moroccan side, the police waved their truncheons and bounced around nervously; the scaling of the fence had showed them up as being ineffective at their job. But on neither side of the fence did the police dare go up. The two shapes were right at the very top of the fence and it was said that they would be intercepted by the relevant police force the second they came down. But the two shapes stubbornly stayed put. The hours passed and the sun burned at its fiercest, warming up the day, and finally the Spanish police decided they'd better do something. So they made their move. They would go up there and force the shapes down, because their powers of persuasion had come to nothing. With a fair amount of effort, because they weren't equipped for such things, a team of officers managed to get quite close to them, close enough to see who and indeed what they were dealing with. Two people draped over the spikes on top of the fence. Who were they?

The scholars never came to Gurugu to analyse the poem and so what Peter's father meant by the third verse remained a mystery. *And godly battle will wage on high.* Was the last line a prophecy or a portrayal of something nobody wished to see? Could *on high* have referred to the rugged crag where Omar and Aliko were summoned to judgement? Or might it have been the top of the spiked fence where those two shapes came to rest?

The search party found the two sick women in the dry riverbed, carried them up the hill and left them just outside the camp, the better to get some respite. When the stamping began, the two women felt the earth pulsating beneath them and they knew something big was happening. They rallied themselves and tried to cry out, so that their brothers, the Africans who had congregated on Gurugu mountain to enter Europe via the Spanish border, the best path available to them, would remember them and include them in their plans. Whether because of their efforts, or because the men who'd left them there hadn't forgotten them in the first place, a group of men eventually came to get them. They had gathered leftover rags and clothing discarded by people who wanted to travel lightly in the coming hours, and using branches and leaves pulled from bushes, they improvised padding to protect their sisters' buttocks and thighs. And then again they left them, there was nothing else for it. The women were in very poor health, they were to rest and wait for the call.

When the call came, everyone stood up and several men carried the two women to the foot of the fence, alternating as they went. It was still dark, but the fence seemed to glow with the faith and conviction of the hundreds of Africans gathered before it. A decision had been made. Given the state the women were in, one of them having suffered a miscarriage, the other having been assaulted, they could not have been left to fend for themselves on the mountain. The omens were ill and the chances of them finding medical help in the Moroccan villages that skirted Gurugu increasingly slim. So it was decided that the women should be taken to the fence, despite their ailing health, and four men carried them on their backs taking turns. They got to the foot of the fence. It was the dead of night. The men tilted back their heads, sizing up the climb to the thorny summit, and then they set off. Going one step at a time, and via a thousand small manoeuvres, with everyone lending a hand and a little strength, they managed to get the two women to the top. The undertaking had pushed everyone to the very limit, because the two women were suffering badly and couldn't hold on to the fence for themselves. But somehow, sweat pouring from them despite the early morning chill, the men got them up. They took hold of each woman's right foot and swung a leg over the top, then they used strips of their clothing and a little rope to hold them in place, to stop them falling. And there the women sat, heads slumped forward, hands splayed to keep the spikes from their faces, one leg either side of the fence, like jockeys in some Dantesque horse race, riding to a party hosted by a mysterious man with hidden features. Their brothers left them there to be recovered by whichever police force and taken to whichever hospital, for the brothers had their own dates with destiny to attend to: they were trying to get to the other side, feeling and really believing that getting there, come what may, was a great victory in itself.

THE BEGINNING AND THE END

I'm African and I was in the same cave as Shania and her husband, the place we called the 'residence' to sweeten the bile in our throats. I heard the stories told there first-hand, but they jumbled together in my mind and I struggled to take everything in once I'd found out about the trade in women. Trade if that's what it can be called, as practised by Aliko and one or two accomplices. I didn't know the other people in the cave and so there are details I was never party to. Indeed, although I had long yearned to reach the other side, I never expected to find myself gathered with so many young Africans in a place that was neither a town nor a village. I wanted there to be a way for those men's stories to be told. I found it fascinating to learn why each one of them had left home, every reason different to the hundreds of others, and yet they'd all, we'd all, decided to set out on a journey we knew nothing about, as if in this day and age there was no way of finding out about where we were heading, whichever country we'd chosen for ourselves. For the first time I realised that what mattered was the ideal, that the ideal was greater than anything else in our lives. It wouldn't have mattered if someone had told us our European lives would actually be worse than the lives we led on the mountain, for the journey itself had come to carry such extraordinary meaning and was therefore unstoppable, for we all know what happens when Africans bring magic into the equation. And I must confess that the ceremony of the pledge made a huge impression on me, because it was as if we'd been sprinkled with a little . . . well, magic. I didn't hear the end of what was said, for my spirit had already surrendered to the sentiment, but even so, I didn't go with them to the fence that day, as I will soon explain. But first I will tell my story.

In the place I was born, you grew up and you were presented with the facts of life: stories set in stone, restrictions long established. If custom dictated something, then that something was fixed, nobody could touch it or change it. This was because, deep down, nobody really knew where things got decided. So you couldn't talk about them. This is the way that so many African things, all of them in fact, are left unsaid. But the story of a continent emptying itself in order to go to another one has to be told, and it has to be told where it's happening, otherwise it would be like a useful object that has two parts and one gets lost: the object would cease to function. You heard me right: a useful object, a tool.

After seeing what happened on the mountain, and having heard stories both profound and pathetic, my own story, the life I'd led before ending up on the mountain, suddenly seemed trivial to me. It shouldn't have done, because just as my camp companions had their reasons for leaving their homelands, I had mine, and just as theirs concerned their inability to explain the mysteries that surrounded them, mine too concerned something I couldn't understand. But it wasn't just that: in my case there was something painful about what I wasn't able to comprehend. As I said before, we Africans rarely know where things get decided, and this not knowing is the biggest reason Africa is emptying, because if you don't know about something, it's that much harder to change it.

Given my geographical origins, nobody could have expected me to end up on Mount Gurugu, because nobody could have expected me to take such a tortuous path. If my own land had spat me out, I'd have ended up in the sea, which was not so very far away, unless you set off in the opposite direction. In other words, if you traced a line from my homeland to Gurugu, it would have had as many twists and turns as the story that prompted me to set out in the first place. It's a story that I still don't understand myself, even if I tell it well, with all the details. But here goes: I was a teacher in a small school in an area that wasn't very developed, in terms of what the world generally considers as developed, although we lived as best we could. I went on explaining things and writing on the blackboard until a new colleague arrived. I won't give his name, but I will say that he was albino. He was a man with a great many philosophical concerns, as if his whole life was spent worrying about the future. In other words, no matter how much we lacked in the here and now, he found holes in which to plant new worries, to add to the troubles of our daily lives. We needed firewood, means to light a fire and ways to protect ourselves from intruders; he asked what would happen if the world's population increased to such a degree that it became unsustainable and caused a catastrophe; he was worried about what the future would entail if the oil ran out, or if the rivers dried up, the most important ones at least. The man was albino, and when he shared his concerns with me and looked at me, I had to look back at him, because that's the way with conversation. I had to try to hold his gaze, but I also had to try not to show that I found it disturbing, because his eyes roved around all over the place and never stayed still. It meant that I never knew when it would be appropriate to drop my gaze, for I didn't want to be discourteous, but I worried that if I held it too long, it would look like I was staring at the frantic dance of his eyeballs, and that too would be rude. Frankly, I didn't know what to do. But the topics he talked of, his concerns, were deep, and he had me as his confidante: there was absolutely nothing I could do to help him with his troubles, but he expressed his concerns earnestly to me, as if unaware of the limits of my capabilities. For the first time I understood that profound and honest men could also be naive, or appear to be. I began to think that the way he advanced his arguments was connected to the inability of his eyes to focus on any one thing, for he was incapable of worrying about what really ought to have concerned him.

We carried on in this way, that man and I, until a number of new students began to arrive at the school, students who were all albinos like him. My first reaction was that it made sense, that he was a man of his race, or race within a race, who'd made a name for himself and so his reputation had inevitably reached the ears of others like him. Or my first reaction was actually nothing: I didn't wonder about or pay any attention to the stream of albino boys and girls arriving at our school, not until the evidence became overwhelming, not until it had become an exodus. Our school had turned into the place where all the albinos in the region sought refuge. Indeed, a dormitory and a dining room and a kitchen and wash facilities were built, so that the children could live their lives right there in the school. At which point I had to ask myself what was happening: Why couldn't those children live with their own families? I needed to know the truth. I looked into it and was told that the path those children had to take between home and school was so long that it had become dangerous for them, and that's why it was decided they should live at the school. Then women had to be brought to cook for them, men to watch over and protect them.

I began to reflect on my colleague's concerns, and on the fact that if you held his gaze, it went elsewhere, and that I'd become anxious because of the way his focus strayed. I ought to reiterate, this was no simple staring into the distance, it was something quite remarkable, and it had always made me think of faraway countries when I talked to him, because his wandering eye made my mind wander too. But the worst of it came when I asked him the obvious questions about why our school had turned into an albino boarding school. What was going on? Well, what was going on awoke me from my slumber, or snapped me out of my stupor, my self-absorption, for that man's dancing eyes were nothing compared to his story, or the story of those albino children, which was essentially the same thing.

It so happened that, according to a science written in no book, or according to traditions not taught or practised in public, it was believed that albino lives had extraordinary qualities, so extraordinary they had to be exploited. So whenever these traditions dictated, people flocked to albino children seeking the benefits of their extraordinary selves. I don't really know how to explain it, and if the wise African scholars had come to the mountain and any of us had dared ask them about it, they would have taken fully five minutes or more just thinking about how to answer. Indeed the first scholar to answer would probably have said that he would prefer to keep his counsel on the subject.

'I didn't know there were certain matters you couldn't reflect on, doctor,' one of the Gurugu inhabitants would have said, surprised.

'It's not quite that, lad. It's just that some matters cannot be trivialised.'

'I'm not asking you to trivialise it, doctor, just clarify it,' the lad would have said, his surprise growing.

'Using reason to try and explain occult phenomena risks trivialising the matter, that's all I meant.'

'Ah, OK, thanks, doctor.'

'I know I haven't resolved your doubts, but believe me, any attempt to do so would only make matters worse.'

In other words, it would have been the hardest thing for even a group of distinguished scholars to explain. They would not have come across the story in any of the books they'd read. Nevertheless, it was a story, a real and painful story.

Told within its precise context, the better that it may be properly understood, the story gives me the same sinking feeling I experienced in my discussions with my colleague. It so happened that in the communities those albinos had been born into there was a coterie of men and women who believed in the occult powers of anything related to albino beings. The belief was so strong that it led people to do things so wicked that for a long time I was unable to speak of them. I saw the consequences for myself one morning when I got to school. The children's cook couldn't speak. The man who opened and closed the school gate and watched over where the albino children slept couldn't speak either. Dozens of people had gathered at the dormitory door and they were speaking, but for all their bluster, nothing they said helped alleviate the pain.

It went like this: it's night time, you know the teacher and you know he's albino, but other than his philosophical concerns, his human needs are the same as anyone else's. You meet him one day and another day you greet him and the next day you see he's missing a hand; he's wounded, but he's conscious and he talks. He tells you a story, full of blood and pain: he was attacked and physically harmed by strangers, and it's a miracle he's still alive; you're sorry, you swallow your saliva and you hope time will heal him. The day passes, other days pass, you feel sorry for him, for his sadness and for the way you can see him making an effort to fix his gaze; you pity his errant eyes. Night comes and you part until the next day and you see him and he's been wounded again; from the stump of his hand, his attackers have now cut up to the elbow, and thank God he was found when he was because life had been spilling out of him, drop by drop. Many weeks pass and he pulls through, but one day you say farewell and he's attacked again and this time he has his foot cut off. He's in great distress after such a devastating injury, but the people who found him acted fast and he will recover, though the road will be long. He heals and he comes in to school on crutches, kindly donated by a convent and tracked down only after a lengthy search. It's by now very difficult for him to exercise his profession, and increasingly painful to watch him trying to hold his wandering gaze. But he recovers and he hobbles around and through great effort he carries on teaching, but one dark night, evil people enter the place he sleeps and with a savage incision they sever off the whole of his remaining arm. He could hardly defend himself, given his disfigurements, and now his fragile body has suffered so terribly that his very survival is in jeopardy. Albinos were so prized by followers of the occult sciences that respectable sums of money were exchanged for large or small pieces of them, pieces of their already unfortunate lives. I found all this out that day. And because my colleague had reached a certain professional standing, he'd proven his extraordinariness, so that vital pieces of him were worth more.

I worked as a teacher and when that attack occurred I was struck by the great incongruity of performing normal teacherly duties on the one hand, and confronting such irrationality on the other. I couldn't think of anything to justify such a state of affairs, and I didn't think I should have to go on witnessing things that, for a long time, I was unable to speak of. I needed another kind of life and I'd need to cross some kind of threshold or travel over a vast plain before I could put into words what happened at the school that night. That's why I left my country and set out on such a tortuous path, the long road to nowhere.

I spent several months living on the banks of a large lake, having fallen in with a group of Congolese who were fleeing their own sorry fate, seeking more tranquil climes. But the banks of the lake were not tranquil enough for me and, as I travelled lightly, I chose to strike out on my own. I decided I needed a new future and the more distance I put between myself and my homeland the better. I continued my journey, crossing whatever nature put in my path, and after many months of wandering, and many brief stints doing various jobs, I ended up on Mount Gurugu – in the residence, where I met many admirable people.

If I'd opened my mouth to tell my tale to the other residents, no one else would have had the chance to speak. Besides, I didn't want to recount anything as painful as my story, given the situation we were in. I didn't think it right that my story, or rather the story of what happened in a school where I'd taught, be told in the residence, even though it was the reason why I was there, the reason I'd abandoned the part of Africa that corresponded to me. I felt I needed some sort of permission to tell it, that something had to happen to make me feel I could tell the story, and that something never happened, so I kept quiet. I think I did right. Talking about that school would have done nothing for the spirit in the camp. So I waited for others to tell their stories and I enjoyed listening to them, especially the ones that brought a little cheer, until the time came to leave the camp.

Let me now tell of the hours that immediately followed the pledge that was sworn on Mount Gurugu. I sat silently in my tent, or lay on my cardboard, until they woke me and told me it was time for the great march. I told them the truth: I wasn't fit enough to join them: I hadn't recovered from the injuries I'd sustained in a previous attempt at scaling the fence, which had ended with the Spanish police refusing to let us get down. There was not much vegetation on the mountain, but I had some knowledge of plant medicine, so I hung around the camp to see if

I could be of any help to those who returned, for I felt sure there would be some. Later, once the sun had risen and it was possible to see, I wandered down to the lower part of Gurugu and from there I saw two bodies on top of the fence. I didn't know what had happened to the others, but I doubted they'd reached Spanish soil. That said, they didn't come back to the mountain. After seeing what remained of the mass scaling, I turned around and went back up the hill, hoping that the police would realise sooner rather than later that those two people weren't up there out of choice. Despairing, I began thinking about how there wasn't enough earth on the whole mountain to dig the tombs the women deserved, if what I feared had happened proved to be true. I decided to abandon the mountain, hoping there was still somewhere on this earth where people had a heart, but the truth is I didn't know where to head, for I'd ended up on Mount Gurugu by following destiny's trail.

So why did I abandon my quest to reach Europe? One day at the camp, just a normal day, we were told we had visitors: a journalist and his cameraman had come to the mountain to interview and film us. The journalist told us they'd sneaked into the forest, for they hadn't known whether they ought to ask permission, and if so, of whom. He'd come to see us, to see what we thought about the fact that we'd left our own countries and ended up on Mount Gurugu, living like lepers. We couldn't all talk at once, so one of the French speakers went first and began to tell the story from his particular perspective.

The journalist went on asking questions, he seemed like a good person, and that brother answered as best he could. But the visit wasn't just the journalist asking questions and us answering them, he also wanted to try and get inside our heads, to try to understand why we persisted in our goal, time and time again. He showed us photos and video footage of attempts to reach the other side, and their results. The French-speaking companion told the journalist his thoughts and we helped him, adding our own opinions. We told the journalist the truth, that we didn't want to go on cursing fate forever, but that we also had many reasons for wanting to leave our respective countries and we weren't yet ready to talk about them. This didn't satisfy him, he couldn't really understand it, but it was the only truth we had. I remember we asked the journalist his name, and he told us he was called Jordi Abolé; if that's not exactly it, it can't be far off. So while we talked, the better to make us understand what lay in store for us, and maybe because he didn't understand our reasons for being there, he switched on his laptop and showed us some video footage and then a newspaper article with a photo of Africans lying sprawled out on a beach.

'Are they dead?'

'Yes. This is the story as it appeared in a Spanish newspaper.'

'Where was this?' we asked.

'Not far from here. A few miles that way.'

'And how did they die?'

He shrugged his shoulders, but we could see he knew more, so we waited for him to regain his composure and tell us.

'The Guardia Civil say they drowned.'

'They were there then, eh?'

'Who?' the journalist asked.

'The Guardia Civil.'

'Yes.'

'Is that what the newspaper says?'

'The newspaper says they drowned, but some people say different.'

We didn't want to bother him, so we left it at that: he asked us a few more questions and then he took his leave. But we'd understood him, you could see it quite clearly in the video footage: they'd been killed. Either that or they'd all suddenly died while swimming to the beach, which was as hard to believe as the official version, that they'd drowned at high sea and washed up on the beach all together. We knew what had happened, and it was a moment of truth for me. They'd been shot. It wasn't the first time a black African had died trying to reach European soil, or even Spanish soil, but it was the first time I'd heard of them being shot. That settled my doubts. In other words – and anyone is free to say whatever they like about it – they simply hadn't been allowed to reach the beach. I know what I saw, and I tried to reason it through, and I remembered other African stories similar to ours. Force your way in and you might not come out in one piece. That was something my people said a lot, and it's true, and if it was said by my people, and by our neighbours, and by the people beyond them, it had to be a truth of some substance, for my people were a long way away in a different country, and it had reached them there.

Previously, I'd thought the problem was that we didn't have papers: we planned to enter Europe without any papers and that wasn't allowed. I had wondered how they expected us to carry papers when we might be travelling by boat and have to swim the last stretch, but now I realised it wasn't really that at all. They didn't kill you for not having papers, that was just the excuse they used.

So I had my moment of truth and that saying from my village stuck in my mind and I said to myself: Okay, they don't want us coming in, we're black, and it must be a terrible bind to issue new papers to someone who's never had them before, so we're not allowed in. And they'd rather shoot us than have us sneak in. On the other hand, I knew one or two, indeed many Africans, had managed to squeeze in through a crack, or slip in through a door left carelessly ajar, and managed not to be thrown out. But given what I now knew, if I managed to get in and not be thrown out, could I still be sure that when I went to the doctor to get help for my injuries, or any other health issues that might arise, he would not inject me with something to bump me off? How could I be sure, for example, that if I fell sick and put myself in the doctor's care, he wouldn't inject me with something to make me permanently impotent? How could I know that at the first opportunity he wouldn't inject our sisters with something to stop them having children? Could I be sure that when I ordered a cup of tea in a café they wouldn't spit in it because I disgusted them so? Could I be sure that when I ordered an orange juice, if I were ever fortunate enough to be able to afford one, they wouldn't blow their noses in it? Do I exaggerate? Not really, not after what I'd seen. I might even have been justified in saying that drinking a cup of coffee in Europe was tantamount to risking your life. That's right, because how could I be sure that if I went on a long journey and stopped at the service station for a coffee they wouldn't put poison in my cup, to free themselves of one more black, given the fear they had of us entering Europe in the first place? If I were to think logically, it would have been impossible to think otherwise, impossible for me not to have lived in constant fear, not after what I'd seen. In other words, I couldn't trust people who had no respect for my life. That's why I decided not to join the mass scaling of the fence that day. Because in the Africa I'm from, the real Africa, the Africa where people are not offended if you enter their village, there are deaths, but it's never so clear who's responsible for them as it was with those brothers on that beach.

I abandoned the mountain, as I said, but as I walked away I had another moment of truth: the sense of resignation among my people was so strong that I'd have no one to accompany me on my return journey. I was as naked as a newborn baby, naked in the sense that I had nothing to offer anyone in order to obtain anything.

Furthermore, I was still hobbling from my injuries. If I was to eat, I had two options: hobble on until I met a fellow paperless, countryless man who might offer me something, if he had anything to eat himself, or tour the souks and houses begging for food, which I'd be unlikely to get, given who I was. There was a third option, but its unpredictable consequences stopped me from following it through: become a delinquent. That's right, steal things, small things, in order to eat, and in the hope of being arrested and taken to prison where, no matter what the conditions, I'd be fed. Or with a bit of luck, or a lot of luck, a lot of lot of luck, be deported to whatever country I said I was from, which would have been my own. However, that would have been a matter for the Moroccan nation itself to decide, a branch of it much more powerful than the forestry police who kept us in line, and I found it hard to imagine that a country with a police force that beat and killed people would bother to repatriate anybody, unless that anybody had a very big name. Becoming a delinquent could easily have cost me a rib, or an arm, a bone in my good foot or even my life, so I rejected the idea.

So I went back to Mount Gurugu. I still rejected the idea of going somewhere I was neither wanted nor awaited, so I made my way, slowly and painfully, to the mountain's southern face, to the side where the lights of nearby Europe do not reach. If one day a story is published that recounts the incidents that occurred during my stay at the residence, then it will be because my circumstances changed and I was able to make the story known. And if then, by some coincidence, any of my companions from the cave happen to read it, they will remember the saying I told them about not rushing to judge the quality of another man's teeth, lest he end up with their whole mouth. But if fate doesn't intervene and, many years from now, an old man with a white beard is found gathering firewood in the Gurugu foothills, let it be known that I chose the southern face, that my gaze was turned towards the River Zambezi.

Dear readers,

As well as relying on bookshop sales, And Other Stories relies on subscriptions from people like you for many of our books, whose stories other publishers often consider too risky to take on.

Our subscribers don't just make the books physically happen. They also help us approach booksellers, because we can demonstrate that our books already have readers and fans. And they give us the security to publish in line with our values, which are collaborative, imaginative and 'shamelessly literary'.

All of our subscribers:

- receive a first-edition copy of each of the books they subscribe to
- are thanked by name at the end of our subscriber-supported books
- receive little extras from us by way of thank you, for example: postcards created by our authors

BECOME A SUBSCRIBER, OR GIVE A SUBSCRIPTION TO A FRIEND

Visit andotherstories.org/subscribe to help make our books happen. You can subscribe to books we're in the process of making. To purchase books we have already published, we urge you to support your local or favourite bookshop and order directly from them – the often unsung heroes of publishing.

OTHER WAYS TO GET INVOLVED

If you'd like to know about upcoming events and reading groups (our foreign-language reading groups help us choose books to publish, for example) you can:

- join the mailing list at: andotherstories.org/join-us
- follow us on Twitter: @andothertweets
- join us on Facebook: facebook.com/AndOtherStoriesBooks
- follow our blog: andotherstoriespublishing.tumblr.com

This book was made possible thanks to the support of:

Aaron McEnery · Aaron Schneider · Abdullah Chowdhury · Ada Gokay · Adam Barnard · Adam Bowman · Adam Butler · Adam Lenson · Adriana Diaz Enciso · Ailsa Peate · Ajay Sharma · Alan McMonagle · Alastair Gillespie · Alastair Laing · Alex Fleming · Alex Ramsey · Alexandra Citron · Alexandra de Verseg-Roesch · Ali Conway · Ali Smith · Alice Firebrace · Alice Fischer · Alice Nightingale · Alison Hughes · Alison Layland · Alison MacConnell · Alison Winston · Allison Graham · Alyse Ceirante · Amanda · Amanda Harvey · Amelia Ashton · Amelia Dowe · Ami Zarchi · Amine Hamadache · Amitav Hajra · Amy Rushton · Ana Hincapie · Andrea Reece · Andrew Gummerson · Andrew Lees · Andrew Marston · Andrew McDougall · Andrew Reece · Andrew Rego · Angela Creed · Angela Everitt · Angus Walker · Anna Corrigan · Anna McKee-Poore · Anna Milsom · Anna Ruehl · Anna Vaught · Anne Carus · Anne Guest · Anne Claire Le Reste · Anne Marsella · Anne Ryden · Annette Hamilton · Annie McDermott · Anonymous · Anonymous · Anonymous · Anonymous · Anthony Brown · Anthony Carrick · Anton Muscatelli · Antonia Lloyd-Jones · Antonia Saske · Antonio de Swift · Antony Pearce · Aoife Boyd · Archie Davies · Arwen Smith · Asako Serizawa · Asher Norris · Ashley Hamilton · Audrey Mash · Avril Marren · Ayca Turkoglu · Barbara & Terry Feller · Barbara Mellor · Barbara Robinson · Beatriz St. John · Becky Woolley · Belynder Walia · Ben Schofield · Ben Thornton · Benjamin Judge · Bernard Devaney · Beth Hore · Bev Thomas · Beverly Jackson · Bianca Duec · Bianca Jackson · Bianca Winter · Bill Fletcher · Blythe Ridge Sloan · Branka Maricic · Brenda Sully · Brendan McIntyre · Briallen Hopper · Brigita Ptackova · Caitlin Halpern · Caitlyn Chappell · Callie Steven · Calum Colley · Candida Lacey · Caren Harple · Carla Carpenter · Carol Laurent · Carolina Pineiro · Caroline Paul · Caroline Picard · Caroline Smith · Caroline Waight · Caroline West · Cassidy Hughes · Catherine Taylor · Catriona Gibbs · Cecilia Rossi · Cecilia Uribe · Cecily Maude · Charles Raby · Charlie Laing · Charlotte Holtam · Charlotte Murrie & Stephen Charles · Charlotte Ryland · Charlotte Whittle · Cheryl Maude · Chia Foon Yeow · China Miéville · Chris Ames · Chris Nielsen · Chris & Kathleen Repper-Day · Chris Stevenson · Christina Moutsou · Christine Brantingham · Christine Ebdy · Christine Luker · Christopher Allen · Christopher Terry · Ciara Ní Riain · Claire Brooksby · Claire Tristram · Claire Williams · Clare Archibald · Clarissa Botsford · Claudia Hoare · Claudia Nannini · Claudio Guerri · Clifford Posner · Clive Bellingham · Colin Burrow · Colin Matthews · Courtney Lilly · Craig Aitchison · Craig Barney · Dan Walpole · Daniel Arnold · Daniel Gallimore · Daniel Gillespie · Daniel Hahn · Daniel Kennedy · Daniel Rice · Daniel Venn · Daniela Steierberg · Darcy Hurford · Dave Lander · Dave Young · Davi Rocha · David Anderson · David Finlay · David Gavin · David Gould · David Hebblethwaite · David Higgins · David Johnson-Davies · David Jones · David Roberts · David Shriver · David Smith · David Travis · Dawn Leonard · Debbie Pinfold · Declan O'Driscoll · Deirdre Nic Mhathuna · Denise Jones · Denise Muir · Diana Fox Carney · Dinah Bourne · Dominick Santa Cattarina · Donna Daley-Clarke · Duncan Clubb · Ed Owles ·

Edward Haxton · Edward Rathke · Elaine Rassaby · Eleanor Dawson · Eleanor Maier · Elie Howe · Elisabeth Cook · Elise Gilbert · Eliza O'Toole · Elizabeth Bryer · Elizabeth Heighway · Ellen Coopersmith · Ellen Kennedy · Ellie Goddard · Elly Zelda Goldsmith · Elsbeth Julie Watering · Emily Taylor · Emily Williams · Emily Yaewon Lee & Gregory Limpens · Emma Bielecki · Emma Louise Grove · Emma Perry · Emma Teale · Emma Timpany · Emma Yearwood · Eric E Rubeo · Erin Grace Cobby · Eva Kostyu · Ewan Tant · Fawzia Kane · Finbarr Farragher · Finlay McEwan · Finnuala Butler · Fiona Quinn · Florian Duijsens · Fran Sanderson · Frances Hazelton · Francesca Brooks · Francesca Fanucci · Francis Taylor · Francisco Vilhena · Frank van Orsouw · Freya Warren · Friederike Knabe · Gabriela Lucia Garza de Linde · Gabrielle Crockatt · Gale Pryor · Gary Gorton · Gavin Collins · Gavin Smith · Gawain Espley · Gemma Tipton · Geoff Thrower · Geoffrey Cohen · Geoffrey Urland · George Christie · George McCaig · George Wilkinson · Georgia Panteli · Gerard Mehigan · Gill Boag-Munroe · Gillian Ackroyd · Gillian Bohnet · Gillian Grant · Gordon Cameron · Graham Duff · Graham R Foster · Grant Hartwell · Grant Rintoul · GRJ Beaton · Hadil Balzan · Hank Pryor · Hannah Jones · Hannah Mayblin · Hannah Richter · Hannah Stevens · Hans Lazda · Harriet Mossop · Harriet Spicer · Hattie Edmonds · Heather Tipon · Helen Asquith · Helen Bailey · Helen Barker · Helen Brady · Helen Collins · Helen Snow · Helen Weir · Helen Wormald · Henrike Laehnemann · Henry Asson · HL Turner-Heffer · Howard Robinson · Hugh Gilmore · Hugh Lester · Iain Munro · Ian Barnett · Ian McMillan · Ian Randall · Ingrid Olsen · Irene Mansfield · Isabel Adey · Isabella Garment · Isabella Weibrecht · J Collins · Jack Brown · Jacqueline Haskell · Jacqueline Lademann · Jacqueline Ting Lin · Jacqueline Vint · James Attlee · James Butcher · James Cubbon · James Lesniak · James Portlock · James Scudamore · James Tierney · James Wilper · Jamie Walsh · Jane Leuchter · Jane Woollard · Janet Sarbanes · Janette Ryan · Janika Urig · Jasmine Gideon · Jean Pierre de Rosnay · Jean-Jacques Regouffre · Jeanne Wilson · Jeff Collins · Jen Campbell · Jennifer Bernstein · Jennifer Higgins · Jennifer O'Brien · Jenny Huth · Jenny Newton · Jenny Yang · Jeremy Faulk · Jeremy Weinstock · Jess Howard-Armitage · Jessica Schouela · Jethro Soutar · Jillian Jones · Jim Boucherat · Jim McAuliffe · Jo Bell · Jo Bellamy · Jo Harding · Jo Lateu · Joanna Flower · Joanna Luloff · Joao Pedro Bragatti Winckler · Jodie Adams · Jodie Hare · Joel Love · Joelle Delbourgo · Joelle Skilbeck · Johan Forsell · Johan Trouw · Johanna Eliasson · Johannes Georg Zipp · John Conway · John Gent · John Hartley · John Hodgson · John Kelly · John McKee · John Royley · John Shaw · John Steigerwald · John Winkelman · Jonathan Blaney · Jonathan Watkiss · Joseph Cooney · Joseph Zanella · Joshua Davis · Joshua McNamara · Judith Virginia Moffatt · Julia Hays · Julia Hobsbawm · Julia Hoskins · Julia Rochester · Julian Duplain · Julian Lomas · Julie Arscott · Julie Gibson · Julie Gibson · JW Mersky · Kaarina Hollo · Kapka Kassabova · Karen Davison · Karen Faarbaek de Andrade Lima · Karen Waloschek · Karl Chwe · Kasper Hartmann · Katarina Trodden · Kate Attwooll · Kate Gardner · Kate Griffin · Katharina Liehr · Katharine Freeman · Katharine Nurse · Katharine Robbins · Katherine El-Salahi · Katherine Green · Katherine Mackinnon · Katherine Parish · Katherine Skala · Katherine Sotejeff-Wilson · Kathleen Magone · Kathryn

Edwards · Kathryn Lewis · Katie Brown · Katrina Thomas · Keith Walker · Kent McKernan · Kirsten Major · KL Ee · Kristin Djuve · Lana Selby · Laura Batatota · Laura Clarke · Laura Lea · Laura Renton · Laura Waddell · Lauren Ellemore · Laurence Laluyaux · Leanne Bass · Leigh Vorhies · Leonie Schwab · Leonie Smith · Leri Price · Lesley Lawn · Lesley Watters · Liliana Lobato · Linda Walz · Lindsay Brammer · Lindsey Ford · Lindy van Rooyen · Liz Sage · Lizzi Thomson · Lizzie Broadbent · Lizzie Coulter · LJ Nicolson · Lochlan Bloom · Lola Boorman · Loretta Platts · Lorna Bleach · Lorna Scott Fox · Lottie Smith · Louisa Hare · Louise Curtin · Louise Musson · Louise Musson · Louise Piper · Luc Verstraete · Lucia Rotheray · Lucile Lesage · Lucy Caldwell · Lucy Hariades · Lucy Moffatt · Lucy Phillips · Luke Healey · Lydia Bruton-Jones · Lynda Graham · Lynn Martin · M Manfre · Madeleine Kleinwort · Madeline Teevan · Maeve Lambe · Maggie Livesey · Maisie Gibson · Mal Campbell · Mandy Wight · Manja Pflanz · Marcella Morgan · Marcia Walker · Margaret Jull Costa · Marie Donnelly · Marina Castledine · Marja S Laaksonen · Mark Lumley · Mark Sargent · Mark Sztyber · Mark Waters · Martha Gifford · Martha Nicholson · Martin Boddy · Martin Brampton · Martin Price · Martin Vosyka · Martin Whelton · Mary Carozza · Mary Wang · Marzieh Youssefi · Matt Chittock · Matt & Owen Davies · Matt Klein · Matthew Armstrong · Matthew Francis · Matthew Geden · Matthew Smith · Matthew Thomas · Matty Ross · Maureen Pritchard · Maurice Maguire · Max Longman · Meaghan Delahunt · Megan Wittling · Melanie Healy · Melissa Beck · Melissa da Silveira Serpa · Melissa Quignon-Finch · Meredith Martin · Merima Jahic · Michael Aguilar · Michael Andal · Michael Johnston · Michael Moran · Michael Ward · Michael John Garcés · Michele Keyaert · Michelle Lotherington · Milo Waterfield · Miranda Persaud · Mitchell Albert · Molly Ashby · Molly Foster · Monika Olsen · Morgan Lyons · N Jabinh · Namita Chakrabarty · Nancy Oakes · Natalie Smith · Nathalie Adams · Nathalie Atkinson · Neil Pretty · Nia Emlyn-Jones · Nicholas Brown · Nick Flegel · Nick James · Nick Nelson & Rachel Eley · Nick Sidwell · Nick Williams · Nicola Hart · Nicola Sandiford · Nicole Matteini · Nikolaj Ramsdal Nielsen · Nina Alexandersen · Nina Moore · Noah Levin · Nuala Watt · Octavia Kingsley · Olivia Payne · Pam Madigan · Pamela Ritchie · Pashmina Murthy · Pat Crowe · Patricia Hughes · Patrick Owen · Paul Cray · Paul Fulcher · Paul Griffiths · Paul Howe & Ally Hewitt · Paul Jones · Paul Munday · Paul Myatt · Paul Robinson · Paul Segal · Paula Edwards · Paula McGrath · Penelope Hewett Brown · Peter McCambridge · Peter Rowland · Peter Vos · Philip Carter · Philip Warren · Phyllis Reeve · Piet Van Bockstal · PM Goodman · Polly Walshe · PRAH Foundation · Rachael Boddy · Rachael Williams · Rachel Bambury · Rachel Beddow · Rachel Gregory · Rachel Hinkel · Rachel Lasserson · Rachel Matheson · Rachel Parkin · Rachel Van Riel · Rachel Wadham · Rachel Watkins · Read MAW Books · Rebecca Braun · Rebecca Moss · Rebecca Rosenthal · Rebekah Hughes · Renee Humphrey · Rhiannon Armstrong · Rhodri Jones · Richard Ashcroft · Richard Bauer · Richard Ellis · Richard Mansell · Richard Priest · Richard Shea · Richard Shore · Rishi Dastidar · Rita Hynes · Robert Downing · Robert Gillett · Robert Hugh-Jones · Robert Norman · Robin Patterson · Robin Taylor · Ros Schwartz · Rose Arnold · Rose Skelton · Roz Simpson · Rupert Ziziros · Ruth Larrea · Ruth Parkin · Sally Baker · Sam Gordon ·

Sam Norman · Sam Ruddock · Sam Stern · Samantha Smith · Sandra Neilson · Sarah Arboleda · Sarah Benson · Sarah Butler · Sarah Duguid · Sarah Jacobs · Sarah Lippek · Sarah Lucas · Sarah Pybus · Sarah Wollner · Sasha Dugdale · Scott Thorough · Sean Malone · Sean McGivern · Seini O'Connor · Shannon Knapp · Shawn Moedl · Sheridan Marshall · Shirley Harwood · Sian Rowe · Sigurjon Sigurdsson · Simon Armstrong · Simon James · Simon Robertson · Siobhan Jones · Sioned Puw Rowlands · SJ Bradley · SK Grout · Sofia Hardinger · Sonia Crites · Sonia McLintock · Sonia Overall · Sophie Bowley-Aicken · Sophy Roberts · ST Dabbagh · Stacy Rodgers · Stefanie Barschdorf · Stefanie May IV · Steph Morris · Stephan Eggum · Stephanie Lacava · Stephen Coade · Stephen Pearsall · Steven Norton · Stu Sherman · Stuart Wilkinson · Sue & Ed Aldred · Sue Little · Susan Higson · Susan Irvine · Susie Roberson · Suzanne Fortey · Suzanne Lee · Suzy Ceulan Hughes · Swannee Welsh · Tamara Larsen · Tammi Owens · Tammy Harman · Tammy Watchorn · Tania Hershman · Ted Burness · Teresa Griffiths · Terry Kurgan · Thees Spreckelsen · Thomas Bell · Thomas Chadwick · Thomas Fritz · Thomas van den Bout · Tiffany Lehr · Tim Theroux · Timothy Harris · Tina Rotherham-Winqvist · Toby Ryan · Todd Greenwood · Tom Darby · Tom Franklin · Tom Gray · Tom Ketteley · Tom Wilbey · Tony Bastow · Torna Russell-Hills · Tracy Northup · Tracy Shapley · Trevor Lewis · Trevor Wald · Val Challen · Vanessa Jones · Vanessa Nolan · Vanessa Rush · Victor Meadowcroft · Victoria Adams · Victoria Walker · Vilis Kasims · Virginia Weir · Visaly Muthusamy · Wendy Langridge · Wenna Price · Will Huxter · Will Nash & Claire Meiklejohn · William Dennehy · William Mackenzie · William Schwaber · William Schwartz · Zoë Brasier · Zoe Stephenson

Current & Upcoming Books

01 Juan Pablo Villalobos, *Down the Rabbit Hole*
translated from the Spanish by Rosalind Harvey

02 Clemens Meyer, *All the Lights*
translated from the German by Katy Derbyshire

03 Deborah Levy, *Swimming Home*

04 Iosi Havilio, *Open Door*
translated from the Spanish by Beth Fowler

05 Oleg Zaionchkovsky, *Happiness is Possible*
translated from the Russian by Andrew Bromfield

06 Carlos Gamerro, *The Islands*
translated from the Spanish by Ian Barnett

07 Christoph Simon, *Zbinden's Progress*
translated from the German by Donal McLaughlin

08 Helen DeWitt, *Lightning Rods*

09 Deborah Levy, *Black Vodka: ten stories*

10 Oleg Pavlov, *Captain of the Steppe*
translated from the Russian by Ian Appleby

11 Rodrigo de Souza Leão, *All Dogs are Blue*
translated from the Portuguese by Zoë Perry & Stefan Tobler

12 Juan Pablo Villalobos, *Quesadillas*
translated from the Spanish by Rosalind Harvey

13 Iosi Havilio, *Paradises*
translated from the Spanish by Beth Fowler

14 Ivan Vladislavić, *Double Negative*

15 Benjamin Lytal, *A Map of Tulsa*

16 Ivan Vladislavić, *The Restless Supermarket*

17 Elvira Dones, *Sworn Virgin*
translated from the Italian by Clarissa Botsford

37 Various, *Lunatics, Lovers and Poets: Twelve Stories after Cervantes and Shakespeare*

38 Yuri Herrera, *The Transmigration of Bodies*
translated from the Spanish by Lisa Dillman

39 César Aira, *The Seamstress and the Wind*
translated from the Spanish by Rosalie Knecht

40 Juan Pablo Villalobos, *I'll Sell You a Dog*
translated from the Spanish by Rosalind Harvey

41 Enrique Vila-Matas, *Vampire in Love*
translated from the Spanish by Margaret Jull Costa

42 Emmanuelle Pagano, *Trysting*
translated from the French by Jennifer Higgins and Sophie Lewis

43 Arno Geiger, *The Old King in His Exile*
translated from the German by Stefan Tobler

44 Michelle Tea, *Black Wave*

45 César Aira, *The Little Buddhist Monk*
translated from the Spanish by Nick Caistor

46 César Aira, *The Proof*
translated from the Spanish by Nick Caistor

47 Patty Yumi Cottrell, *Sorry to Disrupt the Peace*

48 Yuri Herrera, *Kingdom Cons*
translated from the Spanish by Lisa Dillman

49 Fleur Jaeggy, *I am the Brother of XX*
translated from the Italian by Gini Alhadeff

50 Iosi Havilio, *Petite Fleur*
translated from the Spanish by Lorna Scott Fox

51 Juan Tomás Ávila Laurel, *The Gurugu Pledge*
translated from the Spanish by Jethro Soutar

52 Joanna Walsh, *Worlds from the Word's End*

53 César Aira, *The Lime Tree*
translated from the Spanish by Chris Andrews

54 Nicola Pugliese, *Malacqua*
translated from Italian by Shaun Whiteside

55 Ann Quin, *The Unmapped Country*

JUAN TOMÁS ÁVILA LAUREL was born in 1966 in Equatorial Guinea. The Gurugu Pledge is his second novel to appear in English, and follows his 2015 Independent Foreign Fiction Prize-shortlisted debut *By Night the Mountain Burns*, which was based on his memories of growing up on the remote island of Annobón. He made headlines in 2011 by embarking on a hunger strike, in an anti-government protest. He now lives exiled in Barcelona.

JETHRO SOUTAR is a translator of Spanish and Portuguese. He has translated novels from Argentina, Brazil, Portugal and Guinea-Bissau, and his translation of Juan Tomás Ávila Laurel's previous work, *By Night the Mountain Burns*, was shortlisted for the Independent Foreign Fiction Prize. He is a co-founder of Ragpicker Press and Editor of Dedalus Africa. He lives in Lisbon.